"Are you sure you want to be alone in this house tonight?"

His tone altered subtly, sending a prickle of alarm down Arden's spine. "Why? What aren't you telling me?" When he didn't answer immediately, she moved closer, peering into his eyes until he glanced away. "You didn't come over here to clear the air, did you? What's going on, Reid? For the last time, why are you really here?"

He peered past her shoulder into the garden. "You haven't heard, then."

"Heard what?"

His troubled gaze came back to her. "There's been a murder."

KILLER INVESTIGATION

AMANDA STEVENS

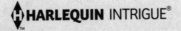

ISBN-13: 978-1-335-60448-4

Killer Investigation

Copyright © 2019 by Marilyn Medlock Amann

HARLEQUIN®
www.Harlequin.com

Amanda Stevens is an award-winning author of over fifty novels, including the modern gothic series The Graveyard Queen. Her books have been described as eerie and atmospheric, "a new take on the classic ghost story." Born and raised in the rural South, she now resides in Houston, Texas, where she enjoys binge-watching, bike riding and the occasional margarita.

Books by Amanda Stevens

Harlequin Intrigue

Twilight's Children

Criminal Behavior
Incriminating Evidence
Killer Investigation

Pine Lake
Whispering Springs

Bishop's Rock (ebook novella)

MIRA Books

The Graveyard Queen

The Restorer
The Kingdom
The Prophet
The Visitor
The Sinner
The Awakening

Visit the Author Profile page at Harlequin.com.

CAST OF CHARACTERS

Arden Mayfair—Her homecoming has awakened a dormant killer driven to relive the ecstasy of his first kill.

Reid Sutton—A powerful enemy is setting him up for murder. Arden claims to have his back, but can he trust her not to run out on him again?

Calvin Mayfair—The scars of his bleak childhood linger.

Clement Mayfair—Arden's cold, taciturn grandfather never gave her the time of day. Now he seems bent on driving a wedge between her and Reid.

Dave Brody—Fresh out of prison, he has an ax to grind with Reid's family.

Boone Sutton—Reid's father warns him about exposing family secrets.

Ginger Vreeland—She disappeared ten years ago without a trace, taking the identity of a killer with her.

Chapter One

The house on Tradd Street hadn't changed much since Arden Mayfair had left home fourteen years ago. The beautiful grand piano still gathered dust at one end of the parlor while a long-dead ancestor remained on guard above the marble fireplace. Plantation shutters at all the long windows dimmed the late-afternoon sunlight that poured down through the live oaks, casting a pall over the once stately room. The echo of Arden's footfalls followed her through the double doors as the oppressive weight of memories and dark tragedy settled heavily upon her shoulders.

Her gaze went to the garden and then darted away. She wouldn't go out there just yet. If she left tomorrow, she could avoid the lush grounds altogether, but already the interior walls were closing in on her. She drew a breath and stared back at her ancestor, unfazed by the flared nostrils and pious expression. She'd never been afraid of the dead. It was the living that haunted her dreams.

She wrinkled her nose as she turned away from the portrait. The house smelled musty from time and neglect, and she would have liked nothing more than to throw open the windows to the breeze. The whole place needed a good airing, but the patio doors were kept closed for a reason.

Berdeaux Place hadn't always been a shuttered mausoleum. The gleaming Greek Revival with its elegant arches and shady piazzas had once been her grandmother's pride and joy, an ancestral treasure box filled with flowers and friends and delectable aromas wafting from the kitchen. When Arden thought back to her early childhood days, before the murder, she conjured up misty images of garden parties and elegant soirees. Of leisurely mornings in the playroom and long afternoons in the pool. Sometimes when it rained, her mother would devise elaborate scavenger hunts or endless games of hide-and-seek. Arden had once sequestered herself so well in the secret hidey-hole beneath the back staircase that the staff had spent hours frantically searching the house from top to bottom while she lay curled up asleep.

After a half-hearted scolding from her mother, Arden had been allowed to accompany her into the parlor for afternoon tea. The women gathered that day had chuckled affectionately at the incident as they spooned sugar cubes into their Earl Grey and nibbled on cucumber sandwiches. Basking in the limelight of their indulgence, Arden had gorged herself on shortbread cookies while stuffing her pockets with macaroons to later share with her best friend. When twilight fell, wrapping the city in shadows and sweet-scented mystery, she'd slipped out to the garden to watch the bats.

It was there in the garden that Arden had stumbled upon her mother's body. Camille Mayfair lay on her back, eyes lifted to the sky as if waiting for the moon to rise over the treetops. Something had been placed upon her lips—a crimson magnolia petal, Arden would later learn. But in that moment of breathless terror, she'd been aware of only one thing: the excited thumping of a human heart.

As Arden grew older, she told herself the sound had been her imagination or the throb of her own pulse. Yet, when she allowed herself to travel back to that twilight, the pulsation seemed to grow and swell until the cacophony filled the whole garden.

It was the sound of a beating heart that had lured her from her mother's prone body to the summerhouse, where a milky magnolia blossom had been left on the steps. The throbbing grew louder as Arden stood in the garden peering up into the ornate windows. Someone stared back at her. She was certain of it. She remained frozen—in fear and in fascination—until a bloodcurdling scream erupted from her throat.

As young as she was, Arden believed that bloom had been left for her to find. The killer had wanted her to know that he would one day come back for her.

Camille Mayfair had been the first known victim of Orson Lee Finch, the Twilight Killer. As the lives of other young, single mothers had been claimed that terrible summer, the offspring left behind had become known as Twilight's Children, a moniker that was still trotted out every year on the anniversary of Finch's arrest. New revelations about the case had recently propelled him back into the headlines, and Arden worried it was only a matter of time before some intrepid reporter came knocking on her door.

So why had she come back now? Why not wait until the publicity and curiosity had died down once again? She had business to attend to, but nothing urgent. After all, months had gone by since her grandmother's passing. She'd certainly been in no hurry to wrap up loose ends. She'd come in for the service, left the same day, and the hell of it was, no one had cared. No one had asked her to stay. Not her estranged grandfather, not her uncle, not the friends and distant relatives she'd left behind long ago.

Her invisibility had been a painful reminder that she didn't belong here anymore. Although Berdeaux Place was hers now, she had no intention of staying on in the city, much less in this house. Her grandmother's attorney was more than capable of settling the estate once Arden had signed all the necessary paperwork. The house would be privately listed, but, with all the inherent rules and regulations that bound historic properties, finding the right buyer could take some time.

So why *had* she come back?

Maybe a question best not answered, she decided.

As she turned back to the foyer to collect her bags, she caught a movement in the garden out of the corner of her eye. She swung around, pulse thudding as she searched the terrace. Someone was coming along one of the pathways. The setting sun was at his back, and the trees cast such long shadows across the flagstones that Arden could make out little more than a silhouette.

Reason told her he was just one of the yard crew hired by the attorney to take care of the grounds. No cause for panic. But being back in this house, wallowing in all those old memories had left her unnerved. She reached for the antique katana that her grandmother had kept at the ready atop her desk. Slipping off the sheath, Arden held the blade flat against the side of her leg as she turned back to the garden.

The man walked boldly up to one of the French doors and banged on the frame. Then he cupped his face as he peered in through one of the panes. "I see you in there," he called. "Open up!"

Arden's grip tightened around the gilded handle. "Who are you? What do you want?"

"Who am I? What the…?" He paused in his incredulity. "Cut it out, Arden. Would you just open the damn door?"

The familiarity of his voice raised goose bumps as she walked across the room to peer back out at him. Her heart tumbled in recognition. The eyes…the nose…that full, sensuous mouth… "Reid?"

His gaze dropped to the weapon in her hand. "Just who the hell were you expecting?"

She squared her shoulders, but her tone sounded more defensive than defiant. "I certainly wasn't expecting you."

"Are you going to let me in or should we just yell through the glass all night?"

She fumbled with the latch and then drew back the door. "What are you doing here anyway? You scared me half to death banging on the door like that."

He nodded toward the blade. "Were you really going to run me through with that thing?"

"I hadn't decided yet."

"In that case…" He took the sword from her hand and brushed past her into the parlor.

"By all means, come on in," she muttered as she followed him back into the room. She clenched her fists as if she could somehow control her racing pulse. He had startled her, was all. Gave her a bad fright leering in through the windows like a Peeping Tom. Her reaction had everything to do with the situation and nothing at all to do with the man. She was over Reid Sutton. He'd been nothing more than a memory ever since she'd left for college at eighteen, determined to put him and Charleston in her rearview mirror. They'd had a grand go of it. Given both families plenty of gray hairs and sleepless nights, and then the adventure had run its course. Arden had needed to get serious about her future and, at eighteen, Reid Sutton had been anything but serious. They'd both had a lot of growing up to do. At least Arden had been mature enough to realize she needed to break away before she made an irrevocable mistake.

She wondered if Reid had ever learned that lesson. She took in his faded jeans, flip-flops and the wavy hair that needed a trim. He was still devastatingly handsome with a smile that could melt the polar ice caps, but she knew better than to succumb to his particular allure. He was still big-time trouble from everything she'd heard, and he still had too much of the rebel in him even at the age of thirty-two. Which was, she suspected, only one of many reasons he'd recently left his family's prestigious but stodgy law firm.

Arden watched him put away the weapon. She had to tear her gaze away from his backside, and that annoyed her to no end. "How did you get into the garden anyway? The side gate is always kept locked." Her grandmother had made certain of that ever since the murder.

He turned with a grin, flashing dimples and white teeth. "The same way you used to sneak out. I climbed up a tree and jumped down over the wall."

She sighed. "You couldn't just ring the doorbell like any normal person?"

"What fun would that be?" he teased. "Besides..." He glanced around. "I wasn't sure you'd be alone."

"So you decided to spy on me instead?"

"Arden, Arden." He shook his head sadly. "Since when did you become so pedestrian? You sound like an old lady. Though you certainly don't present as one." His gaze lingered, making Arden secretly relieved for the Pilates classes and the sleeveless white dress she'd worn to meet her grandmother's attorney. "Just look at you. Thirty-two and all grown-up."

"Which is more than I can say for you." She returned his perusal, taking in the faded jeans and flip-flops.

"It's after-hours, in case you hadn't noticed the time."

"Fair enough. But don't pretend this is our first meeting since I left Charleston. I saw you just six months ago at my grandmother's funeral."

"Yes, but that was from a distance and you were dressed all in black. The hat and veil were sexy as hell, but I barely caught a glimpse of you."

"You could have come by the house after the service."

"I did."

She lifted a brow. "When? I never saw you."

"I didn't come in," he admitted. "I sat out on the veranda for a while."

"Why?"

For a moment, he seemed uncharacteristically subdued. He tapped out a few notes on the piano as Arden waited for his response. The strains of an old love song swirled in her head, tugging loose an unwelcome nostalgia.

"Why didn't you come in?" she pressed.

He hit a sour note. "I guess I wasn't sure you'd want to see me after the way we ended things."

"That was a long time ago."

"I know. But it got pretty heated that last night. I always regretted some of the things I said before you drove off. I didn't even mean most of it."

"Sure you did, but your reaction was understandable. You were angry. We both were. I said some things, too." She shrugged, but inside she was far from cavalier about their current discussion. "I guess it made leaving easier."

"For you maybe."

She cut him a look. "Don't even try to put it all on me. You left, too, remember? That was the agreement. We'd both go off to separate colleges. Do our own thing for a while. Have our own friends. We needed some space. It was all for the best."

"But you never came back."

"That's not true. I came back on holidays and every summer break."

"You never came back to me," he said quietly.

Arden stared at him for a moment and then took a quick glance around. "Are we seriously having this conversation? I feel like I'm being pranked or something."

He didn't bat an eye as he continued to regard her. "You're not being pranked. We're just being honest for once. Airing our grievances, so to speak. Best way to move on."

Arden lifted her chin. "I don't have any grievances, and I moved on a long time ago."

"Everyone has grievances. Without them, there'd be no need for people like me."

"Lawyers, you mean." Her tone sounded more withering than she'd meant it.

He grinned, disarming her yet again. "Grievances are our lifeblood. But to get back on point… Yes, you're right, we did agree to separate colleges. We were supposed to go off and sow our wild oats and then come back to Charleston, settle down, marry and have a few kids, number negotiable."

She gave a quick shake of her head, unable to believe what she was hearing. "When did we ever talk about anything remotely like that?"

"I thought it was understood. In my mind, that was the way it was always supposed to end."

"Is this the part where you tell me you've been pining for me all these years? That I'm the reason you never married?"

"You never married, either," he said. "Have you been pining for me?"

"No, I have not." She planted a hand on one hip as she stared him down. "As fascinating as I'm finding this conversation, I really don't have time for a trip down memory lane. I have a lot of things to do and not much time to do them. So if you'd like to tell me why you're really here..." She tapped a toe impatiently.

"I was hoping we could have dinner some night and catch up."

The suggestion hit her like a physical blow. Dinner? With Reid Sutton? No, not a good idea, ever. The last thing she needed was more drama in her life. All she wanted these days was a little peace and quiet. A safe place where she could reflect and regroup. Her life in Atlanta hadn't turned out as she'd hoped. Not her career, not her personal relationships, not even her friendships. There had been good times, of course, but not enough to overcome the disappointment and humiliation of failure. Not enough to ward off a dangerous discontent that had been gathering for months. None of that needed to be shared with Reid Sutton.

She wandered over to the fireplace, running a finger along the dusty mantel before turning back to him. "What do you call this discussion if it's not catching up?"

"Airing grievances and catching up are two different things." He followed her across the room. "The latter usually goes down better with a cocktail or two. The former sometimes requires a whole bottle."

"The liquor has all been put away," she said. "And as tempting as you make it sound, I'm leaving tomorrow so there's no time for dinner."

He turned to glance back at the foyer where she'd dropped her luggage. "That many suitcases for just one night?"

She shrugged. "I like to be prepared. Besides, I may be going somewhere else after I leave here."

"Where?"

"I haven't decided yet."

He cocked his head and narrowed his gaze. "Is that the best you can do? Disappointing, Arden. You used to be a much better liar."

"I don't have as much practice these days without you egging me on."

His demeanor remained casual, but something dark flashed in his eyes. "As if I ever had to egg you on. About anything."

She felt the heat of an uncharacteristic blush and turned away. "Funny. I don't recall it that way."

"No? I could refresh your memory with any number of specifics, but suffice to say, you were always very good at deception and subterfuge. Better than me, in fact."

"No one was a better liar than you, Reid Sutton."

"It's good to excel at something, I guess. Seriously, though. How long are you really here for? The truth, this time."

She sighed. She could string him along until they

both tired of the game, but what would be the point? "I haven't decided that, either." She brushed off her dusty fingers. "The house needs work before I can list it and I'm not sure I trust Grandmother's attorney to oversee even minor renovations. He's getting on in years and wants to retire." There. She'd owned up to Reid Sutton what she hadn't dared to admit to herself—that she'd come back to Charleston indefinitely.

"Ambrose Foucault still handling her affairs?"

"Yes."

"He's no spring chicken," Reid agreed. "First I'd heard of his retirement, though."

"It's not official. Please don't go chasing after his clients."

He smiled slyly. "Wouldn't dream of it. What about your job? Last I heard you were the director of some fancy art gallery in Atlanta."

"Not an art gallery, a private museum. And not the director, just a lowly archivist."

His eyes glinted. "I bet you ran things, though."

"I tried to, which is why I'm no longer employed there."

"You were fired?"

"Not fired," she said with a frown. "It was a mutual parting of the ways. And anyway, I was ready for a change. You should understand that. Didn't you just leave your father's law practice?"

"Yes, but I *was* fired. Disowned, too, in fact. I'm poor now in case you hadn't heard."

She was unmoved by his predicament. "By Sutton standards maybe. Seems as though I recall a fairly substantial trust fund from your grandfather. Or have you blown through that already?"

"Oh, I've had a good time and then some. But no worries. Provisions have been made for our old age. Nothing on this level, of course." He glanced around the gloomy room with the gilded portraits and price-less antiques. "But we'll have enough for a little place on the beach or a cabin in the mountains. Which do you prefer?"

Arden wasn't amused. The idea that they would grow old together was ludicrous and yet, if she were honest, somehow poignant. "Go away, Reid. I have things to do."

"I could help you unpack," he offered. "At least let me carry your bags upstairs."

"I can manage, thanks."

"Are you sure you want to be alone in this house tonight?"

His tone altered subtly, sending a prickle of alarm down Arden's spine. "Why? What aren't you telling me?" When he didn't answer immediately, she moved closer, peering into his eyes until he glanced away. "You didn't come over here to clear the air, did you? What's going on, Reid? For the last time, why are you really here?"

He peered past her shoulder into the garden. "You haven't heard, then."

"Heard what?"

His troubled gaze came back to her. "There's been a murder."

Chapter Two

"The victim was a young female Caucasian," Reid added as he studied Arden's expression.

She looked suddenly pale in the waning light from the garden, but her voice remained unnervingly calm. "A single mother?"

The question was only natural considering Orson Lee Finch's MO. He'd preyed on young single mothers from affluent families. It was assumed his predilection had been nurtured by contempt for his own unwed mother and resentment of the people he'd worked for. Some thought his killing spree had been triggered by the rejection of his daughter's mother. All psychobabble, as far as Reid was concerned, in a quest to understand the nightmarish urges of a serial killer.

"I don't know anything about the victim," he said. "But Orson Lee Finch will never see the outside of his prison walls again, so this can't have anything to do with him. At least not directly."

Arden's eyes pierced the distance between them. "Why are you here, then? You didn't just come about any old murder."

"A magnolia blossom was found at the scene."

Her eyes went wide before she quickly retreated back into the protection of her rigid composure.

This was the part where Reid would have once taken her in his arms, letting his strength and steady tone reassure her there was no need for panic. He wouldn't touch her now, of course. That wouldn't be appropriate and, anyway, he was probably overreacting. Homicides happened every day. But, irrational or not, he had a bad feeling about this one. He'd wanted Arden to hear about it from him rather than over the news.

She'd gone very still, her expression frozen so that Reid had a hard time reading her emotions. Her hazel eyes were greener than he remembered, her hair shorter than she'd worn it in her younger days, when the sun-bleached ends had brushed her waist. The tiny freckles across her nose, though. He recalled every single one of those.

If he looked closely, he could see the faintest of shadows beneath her eyes and the tug of what might have been unhappiness at the corners of her mouth. He didn't want to look that closely. He wanted to remember Arden Mayfair as that fearless golden girl—barefoot and tanned—who had captured his heart at the ripe old age of four. He wanted to remember those glorious days of swimming and crabbing and catching raindrops on their tongues. And then as they grew older and the hormones kicked in, all those moonlit nights on the beach. The soft sighs and intimate whispers and the music spilling from his open car doors.

The Arden that stood before him now was much too

composed and untouchable in her pristine white dress and power high heels. This Arden was gorgeous and sexy, but too grown-up and far too put together. And here he was still tilting at windmills.

He canted his head as he studied her. "Arden? Did you hear what I said?"

"Yes, I heard you." Her hair shimmered about her shoulders as she tucked it behind her ears. "I'm just not sure what I'm supposed to do with the information."

"You don't have to do anything. I just thought it was something you'd want to know."

"Why?"

"*Why?* Are you really going to make me spell it out?"

"Murder happens all the time, unfortunately, and magnolia blossoms are as common as dirt in Charleston. You said yourself this has nothing to do with Orson Lee Finch."

"I did say that, yes."

"This city has always had a dark side. You know that as well as I do." She glanced toward the garden, her gaze distant and haunted. It wasn't hard to figure out what she was thinking, what she had to be remembering. She'd only been five when she found her mother's body. Reid was a few months older. Even then, he'd wanted to protect her, but they'd been hardly more than babies. Pampered and sheltered in their pretty little world South of Broad Street. The fairy tale had ended that night, but the magic between them had lasted until her car lights disappeared from his view on the night she left town.

No, that wasn't exactly true. If he was honest with himself, their relationship had soured long before that night. The magic had ended when they lost their baby.

But he didn't want to think about that. He'd long since relegated that sad time to the fringes of his memory. Best not to dredge up the fear and the blood and the look on Arden's face when she knew it was over. Best not to remember the panicked trip to the ER or the growing distance between them in the aftermath. The despair, the loneliness. The feeling inside him when he knew it was over.

Reid had learned a long time ago not to dwell on matters he couldn't control. Pick yourself up, dust yourself off and get on with life. Hadn't that been his motto for as long as he could remember? If you pretended long enough and hard enough, you might actually start to believe that you were happy.

In fairness, he hadn't been unhappy. He still knew how to have fun. He could still ferret out an adventure now and then. That was worth something, he reckoned.

With a jolt, he realized that Arden was watching him. She physically started when their gazes collided. Her hand went to her chest as if she could somehow calm her accelerated heartbeat. Or was he merely projecting?

He took a deep breath, but not so deep that she would notice. Instead, he let a note of impatience creep into his voice. "So that's it, then? You're just going to ignore the elephant in the room."

She smoothed a hand down the side of her dress as

if to prove her nonchalance. "What would you have me do?"

"I would expect a little emotion. Some kind of reaction. Not this…" He trailed away before he said something he'd regret.

"Not this what?" she challenged.

He struggled to measure his tone. "You don't have to be so impassive, okay? It's me. You can drop the mask. I just told you that a magnolia blossom was found at the crime scene. Only a handful of people in this city would understand the significance. You and I are two of them."

"White or crimson?"

Finally, a spark. "White. A common variety. Nothing exotic or unusual as far as I've heard. It probably doesn't mean anything. It's not like the killer placed a crimson magnolia petal on the victim's lips. Still…" He paused. "I thought you'd want to know."

Arden's expression remained too calm. "Who was the victim?"

"I told you, I don't know anything about her. The name hasn't been released to the public yet. Nor has the business about the magnolia blossom. We need to keep that to ourselves."

"How do you know about it?"

"I have a detective friend who drops by on occasion to shoot the breeze and drink my whiskey. He sometimes has one too many and let's something slip that he shouldn't."

"What does he think about the murder?" Arden asked. "Do they have any suspects yet?"

"He's not working the case. His information is secondhand. Police department gossip. The best I can tell, Charleston PD is treating it like any other homicide for now."

"For now." She walked over to the French doors and leaned a shoulder against the frame. Her back was to him. He couldn't help admiring the outline of her curves beneath the white dress or the way the high heels emphasized her toned calves. Arden had always been a looker. A real heartbreaker. No one knew that better than Reid.

She traced her reflection in the glass with her fingertip. "When did it happen?"

"The body was found early this morning in an alleyway off Logan." Only half a block from Reid's new place, but for some reason, he didn't see fit to mention that detail. There were a few other things he hadn't shared, either. He wasn't sure why. He told himself he wanted to keep the meeting simple, but when had his feelings for Arden Mayfair ever been simple?

She dropped her hand to her side as she stared out into the gathering dusk. Already, the garden beyond the French doors looked creepy as hell. The statues of angels and cherubs that her grandmother had collected had always been a little too funereal for Reid's tastes. The summerhouse, though. He could see the exotic dome peeking through the tree limbs. The Moroccan structure conjured images of starry nights and secret kisses. He and Arden had made that place their own despite the bad memories.

"Reid?"

He shook himself back to the present. "Sorry. You were saying?"

"The cabdriver had the radio on when I came in from the airport. There wasn't a word of this on the news. No mention of a homicide at all. Ambrose didn't say anything about it, either."

"No reason he would know. As I said, the details haven't yet been released. With all the Twilight Killer publicity recently, the police don't want to incite panic. Keeping certain facts out of the news is smart."

Arden turned away from the garden. "What do you think?"

"About the murder?"

"About the magnolia blossom."

Reid hesitated. "It's too early to speculate. The police are still gathering evidence. The best thing we can do is wait and see what they find out."

The hazel eyes darkened. "Since when have you ever waited for anything?"

I waited fourteen years for you to come back. "I have no choice in the matter. I don't have the connections or the clout I had when I was with Sutton & Associates. All I can do is keep my eyes and ears open. If my friend lets anything else slip, I'll let you know."

She regarded him suspiciously. "You're saying all the right things, but I don't believe you."

"You think I'm making this up?"

"No. I think you came over here for a reason, but it wasn't just to tell me about a murder or to suggest we wait and see what the cops uncover. You're right. Only a handful of people would remember that a white magnolia blossom was left on the summerhouse steps the night my mother was murdered. Everyone else, including the police, focused on the crimson petal placed on her lips—the kiss of death that became the Twilight Killer's signature. The creamy magnolia blossom was never repeated at any of the other murder scenes. Which means it was specific to my mother's death."

"That's speculation, too. We've never known that for certain."

"It's what we always believed," she insisted. "Just like we became convinced that the real killer remained free."

"We were just dumb kids," Reid said. "What were we—all of twelve—when we decided Orson Lee Finch must be innocent? No proof, no evidence, nothing driving our theory but boredom and imagination. We let ourselves get caught up in a mystery of our own making that summer."

"Maybe, but we learned a lot about my mother's case and about how far we were willing to push ourselves to uncover the truth. Don't you remember how dedicated we were? We sat in the summerhouse for hours combing through old newspaper accounts and scribbling in notebooks. We even rode our bikes over to police headquarters and demanded to speak with one of the detectives who had worked the Twilight Killer case."

"For all the good that did us," Reid said dryly. "As I recall, we were not so politely shown the door."

"That didn't stop us though, did it?" For the first time, her eyes began to sparkle as she recalled their ardent pursuit of justice. The polished facade dropped and he glimpsed the girl she'd once been, that scrawny, suntanned dynamo who'd had the ability to wrap him around her little finger with nothing more than a smile.

"No, it didn't stop us," he agreed. "When did anything ever stop us?"

She let that one pass. "We decided the white magnolia blossom represented innocence, the opposite of the bloodred petal placed on my mother and the other victims' lips. Given the Twilight Killer's contempt for single mothers, he would have viewed all of them as tainted and unworthy, hence the crimson kiss of death."

In spite of himself, Reid warmed to the topic. "You were the innocent offspring. The first Child of Twilight."

She nodded. "The white blossom not only represented my virtue, but it was also meant as a warning not to follow in my mother's sullied footsteps."

They shared a moment and then both glanced quickly away. The memory of what they'd created and what they'd lost was as fleeting and bittersweet as the end of a long, hot summer.

"No one knew about the baby," he said softly.

Her gaze darted back to him. "Of course, someone knew. Someone always knows. Secrets rarely stay hidden."

"It never needed to be a secret. Not as far as I was concerned. But…" He closed his eyes briefly. "Water under the bridge. This murder has nothing to do with what happened to us. To you."

"If you believed that, you wouldn't be here."

"Arden—"

"I know why you're here, Reid. I know you. You won't come right out and say it, but you've been dancing around the obvious ever since you got here. Despite what you said earlier, this does involve Orson Lee Finch. The way I see it, there can only be two explanations for why a magnolia blossom was left at that murder scene. Either Finch really is innocent or we're dealing with someone who has been influenced by him. A copycat or a conduit. Maybe even someone with whom he's shared his secrets."

Reid stared at her in astonishment. "You got all that out of what I just told you? That's quite a leap, Arden."

"Is it? Can you honestly say the thought never crossed your mind?"

"You're forgetting one extremely important detail. No red magnolia petal found on the body. No crimson kiss of death placed on the lips. This isn't the work of a copycat and I seriously doubt that a dormant serial killer has suddenly been reawakened after all these years. A jury of Finch's peers found him guilty and none of his appeals has ever gone anywhere. This has to be something else."

Arden refused to back down. "Then I repeat, why are you here?"

He ran fingers through his hair as he tried to formulate the best answer. "Damned if I know at the moment."

She regarded him with another frown. "Just consider the possibility that you and I were right about Orson Lee Finch's innocence. The monster who killed all those women, including my mother, has remained free and well disguised all these years. Maybe I'm the reason he's suddenly reawakened. Maybe the white magnolia blossom left at the crime scene was meant as another warning."

"It's way too early to head down that road," Reid said. "If anything, we may be dealing with a killer who wants to throw the police off his scent."

"So you don't think my coming home has anything to do with this?"

"You just got in today. The murder occurred sometime last night or early this morning."

"A coincidence, then."

"What else could it be?"

She sighed in frustration. "I don't understand you, Reid Sutton. You berate me when I don't show the proper reaction to your revelation about the magnolia blossom, and now you go out of your way to try and convince me—and yourself—that it has nothing to do with me. You came all the way over here just to tell me about a coincidence."

"I'm just trying to be sensible," Reid said.

"You were never any good at that."

"Maybe not, but someone needs to put on the brakes before we get too carried away."

"Now who's being pedestrian?" She brushed back her hair with a careless shrug. "Something's not right about all this. Something's not adding up. Why do I get the feeling you're still holding out on me?"

Reid glanced away. The proximity of the crime scene to his place niggled. Another coincidence, surely, but ever since he'd heard about the murder, he hadn't been able to shake a dark premonition. For days he'd had the feeling that his house was being watched. He'd caught sight of someone lurking in the shadows across the street. One night he'd heard the knob at the back door rattle.

The incidents had started at about the time Dave Brody had been released from prison. The ex-con had stopped by the office as soon as he'd hit town, strutting like a peacock with his smirks and leers and ominous tattoos. He blamed his incarceration on Sutton & Associates, claiming the attorneys that had represented him pro bono—in particular, Reid's father, Boone Sutton—had suppressed a witness that could have corroborated Brody's alibi.

Why he hadn't gone straight to the source of his resentment, Reid didn't know. He hadn't even been out of law school when Brody had been sent up, had only worked peripherally on the appeals. Yet he was apparently the attorney Dave Brody had decided to target for the simple reason that Reid was now the most vulnerable. Without the money and prestige of the firm backing him, he was the easiest to get to. Knock out the son in order to get to the father. But Brody would find out the hard way that Boone Sutton didn't cave so easily, even when family was involved.

Reid hadn't reported the incidents because police involvement would only provoke a guy like Brody. It wasn't the first time and it wouldn't be the last time an irate client had harassed him. Best just to ignore the creep, but still the location of that murder scene bothered him.

"Look, to be honest, I don't know what any of this means," Reid said. "I just knew that I wanted you to hear about that magnolia blossom from me."

He expected another argument; instead, she nodded. "Okay. Thank you. I mean it. I haven't been gracious about any of this. You caught me off guard. That's my only excuse."

"I understand."

"I'm not usually like this. It's just…" She seemed at a loss. "You and I have a complicated history."

"To put it mildly," he agreed.

She drew a breath. "Fourteen years is a long time and yet here we are, back where it all started."

He smiled. "History repeating."

"God, I hope not."

"I'll try not to take that personally."

"You know what I mean. Everything was so intense back then. So life and death. I don't think I could take all that drama these days."

"That's why we have booze. Adulthood has its perks."

"I don't want to numb myself," Arden said with a reproving glance. "But a little peace and quiet would be nice."

"You'll have that in spades here," he said as his gaze traveled back into the foyer. "Are you sure I can't help you with those bags?"

"I can manage."

He lingered for a moment longer, letting his senses drink her up as memories flowed. Man, they'd had some good times together. He hadn't realized until that moment how much he'd missed her. Arden Mayfair wasn't just his ex-girlfriend. She'd been his best friend, his soul mate, and a true and enthusiastic partner in crime. He hadn't had anyone like her in his life since she'd left town. Oh, he had plenty of friends, some with benefits, some without. He never lacked for companionship, but there was no one like Arden. Maybe there never would be.

"I guess I'll say good-night then." He wondered if she noticed the hint of regret in his voice.

"Reid?" She crossed the room quickly and stood on tiptoe to kiss his cheek. She was like quicksilver in his arms, airy and elusive. Before he had time to catch his breath, she'd already retreated, leaving the scent of her honeysuckle shampoo to torment his senses.

He caught her arm and drew her back to him, brushing her lips and then deepening the kiss before she could protest. "Welcome home, Arden."

She looked stunned. "Good night, Reid."

Chapter Three

Arden finished unpacking and then took a quick shower, dressing in linen pants and a sleeveless top before going back downstairs to decide about dinner. There was no food in the house, of course. No one had been living in Berdeaux Place since her grandmother's passing. She would need to make a trip to the market, but for now she could walk over to East Bay and have a solitary meal at her favorite seafood place. Or she could unlock the liquor cabinet and skip dinner altogether. She was in no hurry to venture out now that twilight had fallen.

At loose ends and trying to avoid dwelling on Reid's visit, she wandered through the hallways, trailing her fingers along dusty tabletops and peering up into the faces of forgotten ancestors. Eventually she returned to the front parlor, where her grandmother had once held court. Arden had a vision of her now, sitting ramrod straight in her favorite chair, teacup in one hand and an ornate fan in the other as she surveyed her province with quiet satisfaction. No matter the season or temperature, Evelyn Mayfair always dressed in sophisticated black.

Maybe that was the reason Arden's mother had been drawn to vivid hues, in particular the color red. Arden supposed there was irony—or was it symmetry?—in the killer's final act of placing a crimson petal upon her lips.

Enough reminiscing.

If she wasn't careful, she could drown in all those old memories.

Crossing over to the French doors, she took a peek out into the gardens. The subtle glow from the landscape lighting shimmered off the alabaster faces of the statues. She could hear the faint splash of the fountain and the lonely trill of a night bird high up in one of magnolia trees. Summer sounds that took her back to her early childhood days before tragedy and loss had cast a perpetual shroud over Berdeaux Place.

Checking the lock on the door, she turned away and then swung back. Another sound intruded. Rhythmic and distant.

The pound of a heartbeat was her first thought as her own pulse beat an uneasy tattoo against her throat.

No, not a heartbeat, she realized. Something far less sinister, but invasive nonetheless. *A loose shutter thumping in the breeze most likely. Nothing to worry about. No reason to panic.*

She took another glance into the garden as she reminded herself that her mother had been murdered more than twenty-five years ago. It was unreasonable and perhaps paranoid to think that the real killer had waited all these years to strike again. Reid was right. The magnolia blossom found at the murder scene couldn't be anything more than a coincidence.

Arden stood there for the longest time recounting his argument as she tried to reassure herself that everything was fine. A jury of Finch's peers had found him guilty beyond a reasonable doubt. He would never again be a free man. And even if another killer did prowl the streets, Arden was as safe here as she was anywhere. The property was sequestered behind brick walls and wrought-iron gates. The house had good locks and, ever since the murder, a state-of-the-art security system that had been periodically updated for as long as she could remember. She was safe.

As if to prove to herself that she had nothing to fear, she turned the dead bolt and pushed open the French doors. The evening breeze swept in, fluttering the curtains and scenting the air with the perfume of the garden—jasmine, rose and magnolia from the tree that shaded the summerhouse. She'd smelled those same fragrances the night she'd found her mother's body.

She wouldn't think about that now. She wouldn't spoil her homecoming with old nightmares and lingering fears. If she played her cards right, this could be a new beginning for her. A bolder and more exciting chapter if she didn't let the past hold her back.

Bolstering her resolve, she walked down the flagstone path toward the summerhouse. The garden had been neglected since her grandmother was no longer around to browbeat the yard crew. In six months of Charleston heat and humidity the beds and hedges had exploded. Through the untrimmed canopy of the magnolias, the summerhouse dome rose majestically, and to the left Arden could see the slanted glass roof of the greenhouse.

The rhythmic thud was coming from that direction. The greenhouse door had undoubtedly been left unsecured and was bumping in the breeze.

Before Arden lost her nerve, she changed course, veering away from the summerhouse and heading straight into the heart of the jungle. It was a warm, lovely night and the garden lights guided her along the pathway. She detected a hint of brine in the breeze. The scent took her back to all those nights when she'd shimmied down the trellis outside her bedroom window to meet Reid. Back to the innocent kisses in the summerhouse and to those not so innocent nights spent together at the beach. Then hurrying home before sunup. Lying in bed and smiling to herself as the light turned golden on her ceiling.

Despite the dark shadow that had loomed over the house since her mother's murder, Arden had been happy at Berdeaux Place, thanks mostly to Reid. He'd given her a way out of the gloom, an escape from the despair that her grandmother had sunk more deeply into year after year. Evelyn Berdeaux Mayfair had never gotten over the death of her only daughter and sometimes Arden had wondered if her presence had been more of a curse than a blessing, a constant reminder of what she'd lost.

Her grandmother's desolation had worn on Arden, but Reid had always been there to lift her up. He'd been her best friend, her confidant, and for a time she'd thought him the love her life. Everything had changed that last summer.

Too soon, Arden. Don't go there.

There would be time enough later to reflect on what might have been.

But already wistfulness tugged. She paused on the flagstones and inhaled sharply, letting the perfume of the night lull her. A moth flitted past her cheek as loneliness descended. It had been a long time since she'd felt so unmoored. She blamed her longing on Reid's unexpected visit. Seeing him again had stirred powerful memories.

Something darted through the trees and she whirled toward the movement. She'd been so lost in thought she hadn't kept track of her surroundings, of the danger that had entered the garden.

She stood frozen, her senses on full alert as she tried to pinpoint the source of her unease. The thumping had stopped, and now it wasn't so much a sound or a smell that alarmed her but a dreaded certainty that she was no longer alone.

Her heart started to pound in fear as she peered through the darkness. The reflection of the rising moon in the glass ceiling of the greenhouse cast a strange glow directly over the path where someone stood watching her.

In that moment of terror, Arden wanted nothing so much as to turn and run from the garden, to lock herself away in Berdeaux Place as her grandmother had done for decades. She could grow old in that house, withering away with each passing year, lonely and desolate yet safe from the outside world. Safe from the monster who had murdered her mother and would someday return for her.

She didn't run, though. She braced her shoulders and clenched her fists even as she conjured an image of her own prone body on the walkway, with blood on the flagstones and a crimson magnolia petal adorning her cold lips.

"Arden?"

The voice was at once familiar and strangely unsettling, the accent unmistakably Charleston. A thrill rippled along her backbone. She had lots of videos from her childhood. Her mother had pronounced her name in that same dreamy drawl. *Ah-den.*

He moved out of the shadows and started down the path toward her. Arden stood her ground even as her heart continued to flail. The man was almost upon her before recognition finally clicked. "Uncle Calvin?"

"I'm sorry. I didn't mean to frighten you," he said in his elegant drawl.

"No, it's okay. I just… I wasn't expecting anyone to be out here."

"Nor was I. You gave me quite the start, too, seeing you there in the moonlight. You look so much like your mother I thought for a moment I was seeing her ghost."

For some reason, his observation sent another shiver down Arden's spine.

As he continued toward her, she could pick out the familiar Mayfair features—the dimpled chin and piercing blue eyes melding seamlessly with the Berdeaux cheekbones and nose. Arden had the cheekbones and nose, but her hair wasn't quite so golden and her complexion was far from porcelain. Her hazel eyes had come from her father, she'd long ago decided. A frivolous charmer who'd skipped town the moment he'd learned she was on the way, according to her grandmother. Still, the resemblance was undeniable.

"Ambrose told me a few days ago that you were coming, but somehow it slipped my mind," her uncle said. "I'm so used to letting myself in through the garden gate I never even thought to stop by the house first." He came to a halt on the path, keeping distance between them as if he were worried he might startle her away. "I hope I didn't frighten you too badly."

"It's not you." She let out a breath as she cast a glance into the shadows. "It's this place. After all these years, the garden still unnerves me."

"I'm not surprised." His hair looked nearly white in the fragile light as he thrust it back from his forehead. He was tall, slender and somehow stylish even in his casual attire. In her younger years, Arden had thought her uncle quite dashing with his sophisticated demeanor and mysterious ways. She had always wanted to know him better, but his remoteness had helped foster his mystique. "Even after all these years, the ghosts linger," he murmured.

"You feel it, too," Arden said with a shudder.

"No matter the time of day or year." He paused with a wan smile. "You were so young when it happened. I'm surprised you still feel it so strongly."

"It's not something you ever get over."

"No, I suppose not. I was away at the time. Father

and I had had a falling out so I didn't find out until after the funeral. Maybe that's why the impact only hit me later. I'm sorry I wasn't around to at least offer some comfort."

"I had Grandmother."

"Yes. I remember hearing how she clung to you at the funeral. You were her strength."

"And she, mine, although I don't remember much about that day. It passed in a haze."

"Probably for the best." He gave her another sad smile. "So here you are. Back after all these years."

"Yes."

"It's been a long time. Everyone had begun to think that we'd lost you for good."

Arden wondered whom he included in that "everyone." Not her grandfather, surely. Clement Mayfair had never shown anything but a cursory concern for her welfare. "I've returned periodically for visits. I spent almost every Christmas with Grandmother."

"And now you've come home to any empty house and me looking like something the cat dragged in. I apologize for my appearance," he said as he held up his gloved hands. "I've been working in the greenhouse."

He looked nothing short of pristine. "At this hour?" Arden asked in surprise.

"Maybe you'd like to see what I've been up to. That is, if you don't mind the general disrepair. The greenhouse is in rather a dismal state so mind your step."

"What have you been working on?"

His eyes gleamed in the moonlight. "You'll see."

He turned and she fell into step behind him on the

flagstone pathway, following his graceful gait through borders of silvery artemisia and pale pink dianthus. She felt safe enough in the company of her uncle. She didn't know him well, but he'd always been kind. Still, she couldn't help glancing over her shoulder. She couldn't help remembering that her mother had been murdered on an evening such as this.

The greenhouse door opened with a squeal.

"The hinges have rusted and the latch doesn't catch like it should," he said. "Not that there's anything of value inside. The tools, what's left of them, are secured in the shed around back. The lock needs to be replaced, regardless. No one needs to be traipsing about inside. Could be a lawsuit waiting to happen."

"Ambrose should have had that taken care of," Arden said. "At any rate, I'll have someone come out as soon as possible."

Her uncle glanced over his shoulder. "You're here to stay then."

"I don't know. I haven't made any plans yet."

He looked as if he were on the verge of saying something else, but he shrugged. "You've plenty of time. There's no need to rush any decisions."

She stepped through the door and glanced around. The tables and racks were nearly empty except for a few chipped pots.

"Straight ahead," he said as he peeled off his gloves and tossed them aside.

"I'd nearly forgotten about this place." Arden glanced up in wonder through the glass panels where a few stars had begun to twinkle. "Grandmother never talked about it anymore and we didn't come out here on any of my visits. She gave up her orchids long ago. I'm surprised she didn't have the structure torn down."

"It served a purpose," Calvin said.

"You're being very mysterious," Arden observed.

"Just you wait."

Arden hugged her arms around her middle. "When I was little, Grandmother used to let me come in here with her while she mixed her potions and boosters. Her orchids were the showstoppers at every exhibit, but secretly I always thought they were the strangest flowers with the spookiest names. Ghost orchid, fairy slipper, Dracula benedictii. They were too fussy for my taste. Required too much time and effort. I adored Mother's cacti and succulents. So hardy and yet so exotic. When they bloomed, the greenhouse was like a desert oasis."

"I can imagine."

Arden sighed. "The three of us spent hours in here together, but Grandmother lost interest after the—after Mother was gone. She hired someone to take care of the plants for a while... Eventually everything died."

"Not everything." Her uncle's blue eyes glinted in reflected moonlight. He stepped aside, leaning an arm on one of the tables as he waved her forward. "Take a look."

Arden moved around him and then glanced back. "Is that...it can't be Mother's cereus? It's nearly to the ceiling!" She trailed her gaze up the exotic cactus. "You kept it all this time?"

"Evelyn kept it," he said, referring to his mother and Arden's grandmother by her given name. "After you moved away, it was the only thing of Camille's she had left. She spent most of her time out here, trimming and propagating. As you said, mixing her potions and boosters. She may have lost interest in the orchids, but she never lost her touch."

Arden felt a twinge of guilt. She could too easily picture her grandmother bent to her work, a slight figure, wizened and withered in her solitude and grief. "I see lots of buds. How long until they open?"

"Another few nights. You're lucky. It's promising to be quite a show this year."

"That's why you're here," Arden said. "You've been coming by to take care of the cereus."

"I couldn't let it die. Not after Evelyn had nurtured it all those years. A Queen of the Night this size is rare in these parts and much too large to move. Besides, this is its home."

He spoke in a reverent tone as if concerned for the plant's sensibilities. That was nonsense, of course, nothing but Arden's overstimulated imagination; yet she couldn't help sneaking a glance at her uncle, marveling that she could look so much like him and know so little about him.

Arden's grandparents had divorced when their children were still young. Calvin had remained in the grand old mansion on East Bay Street with Clement Mayfair while his older sister, Camille—Arden's mother—had gone to live with Evelyn at Berdeaux Place. Outwardly, the divorce had been amicable; in reality, a simmering bitterness had kept the siblings apart.

Growing up, Arden could remember only a handful of visits from her uncle and she knew even less about her grandfather, a cold, taciturn man who disapproved of little girls with dirty fingernails and a sense of adventure. On the rare occasions when she'd been summoned to Mayfair House, she'd been expected to dress appropriately and mind her manners, which meant no fidgeting at the dinner table, no speaking unless spoken to.

Clement Mayfair was a tall, swarthy man who had inherited a fortune and doubled it by the time he was thirty. He was in shipping, although to this day, Arden had only a vague idea of what his enterprises entailed. His children had taken after their mother. In her heyday, Evelyn Berdeaux had been a blonde bombshell. Capricious and flirtatious, she must have driven a reclusive man like Clement mad at times. No wonder the marriage had ended so acrimoniously. Opposites might attract, but that didn't make for an easy relationship. On the other hand, Arden and Reid had been so much alike there'd been no one to restrain their impulses.

Her uncle watched her in the moonlight. He had the strangest expression on his face. "Is something wrong?" Arden asked.

Her voice seemed to startle him out of a deep reverie. "No, of course not. I just can't get over how much you look like your mother. Sometimes when you turn your head a certain way…" He trailed off on a note of wonder. "And it's not just your appearance. Your mannerisms, the way you pronounce certain words. It's really remarkable considering Camille died when you were so young."

"That's interesting to know."

He seemed not to hear her. "My sister was full of sunshine and life. She considered each day a new adventure. I was in awe of her when we were children. I sense that quality in you, too, although I think you view each day as something to be conquered," he said with a smile. "Evelyn always said you were a handful."

Arden trailed her finger across one of the scalloped leaves of the cereus. "I suppose I did give her a few gray hairs, although I'm sure she had her moments, too. She became almost a shut-in after Mother died, but I remember a time when she loved to entertain. She kept the house filled with fascinating people who'd traveled to all sorts of glamorous places. It was a bit like living in a fairy tale."

Her uncle remained silent, gazing down at her in the moonlight as if he were hanging on her every word.

"Did you know that she used to organize blooming socials for Mother's cereus? The buds would never open until well past my bedtime, but I was allowed to stay up on the first night to watch the first blossom. The unfurling was magical. And that heavenly scent." Arden closed her eyes and drew a deep breath. "I remember it so well. Not too sweet or cloying, more like a dark, lush jungle."

"I have cuttings at my place and I still do the same," Calvin said. "My friends and I sit out on the balcony with cameras and mint juleps. There's something to be said for Southern traditions. You should join us this year." His voice sounded strained and yet oddly excited.

"At Mayfair House?" Somehow Arden couldn't

imagine her prim and proper grandfather being a party to such a frivolous gathering.

"I haven't lived at Mayfair House in years. I have a place near my studio."

"Your studio?"

His smile turned deprecating. "I paint and sculpt. I dabble a bit in pottery. I even manage to sell a piece now and then."

She put a hand to her forehead. "Of course. You're an artist. I don't know how I let that slip my mind. I'm afraid I haven't been very good at keeping in touch."

"None of us has. We're a very strange family in that regard. I suppose we all like our secrets too much."

Arden couldn't help wondering about his secrets. He was a handsome man, still young at forty-six and ever so charming in manner and speech. Yet now that she was older, the drawl seemed a little too affected and his elegance had a hint of decadence that hadn't aged well. Maybe she was being too critical. Looking for flaws to assuage her conscience. No one on either side of the family had been more distant or secretive than she. Her grandmother had given her a home and every advantage, and Arden had repaid that kindness with bimonthly phone calls and Christmas visits.

As unsatisfied as she'd been with her professional life in Atlanta, she was even more discontent with her personal growth. She'd been selfish and entitled for as long as she could remember. Maybe that assessment was also too critical, but Arden had reached the stage of her life, a turning point, where hard truths needed to be faced. Maybe that was the real reason she'd come back to Charleston. Not to put old ghosts to rest, but to take stock and regroup.

Her uncle picked up a pair of clippers and busied himself cleaning the blades with a tattered rag and some rubbing alcohol. "You know the story of your grandparents' divorce," he said. "I stayed with Father and Camille came here with Evelyn. We lived only blocks apart, yet we became strangers. She blamed Father for the estrangement, but Evelyn could be just as contentious. She had her secrets, too," he added slyly as he tested the clippers by running his finger along the curved blades. Then he hung them on the wall and put away the alcohol.

Arden watched him work. His hands were graceful, his fingers long and tapered, but his movements were crisp and efficient. She marveled at the dichotomy. "No matter who was at fault, it was wrong to keep you and my mother apart. To force you to choose sides. She never wanted that. She used to tell me stories of how close the two of you were when you were little. I know she missed you."

"And yet she never reached out."

"Did you?"

He shrugged good-naturedly. "That's a fair point. Fear of rejection is a powerful deterrent. After the divorce, I'd sneak away from my father's house and come here every chance I got. Sometimes I would just sit in the garden and watch my mother and sister through the windows. Or I'd lie in the summerhouse and stare up at the clouds. Berdeaux Place was like a haven to me back then. A secret sanctuary. Even though Mayfair House has a multitude of sunlit piazzas with breathtaking views of the sea, it seemed a gloomy place after the divorce. It was like all the joy had been stolen and brought here to this house."

"You must have been lonely after they left." Arden knew loneliness, the kind of killing emptiness that was like a physical ache. She'd felt it often in this house and even more so in Atlanta. She felt it now thinking about Reid Sutton.

She brushed back her hair as she glanced up at the sky, trailing her gaze along the same twinkling stars that she and Reid had once counted together as children.

You see that falling star, Arden? You have to make a wish. It's a rule.

I already made a wish. But if I tell you, it won't come true.

That's dumb. Of course, it'll come true.

All right, then. I wish that you and I could be together forever.

That's a stupid thing to wish for because we will be. Promise?

Promise. Now hurry up and make another wish. Something important this time. Like a new bike or a pair of Rollerblades.

"Arden?"

She closed her eyes and drew another breath. "Yes?"

"Where did you go just now? You seemed a million miles away."

"Just lost in thought. This place takes me back."

"That's not a bad thing. Memories are how we keep those we've lost with us always. I made my peace with Evelyn before she passed. I'm thankful for that. And

I'm thankful that you're back home where you belong. Perhaps I'm overstepping my bounds, but I can't help wondering…" He trailed away on a note of uncertainty.

"What is it?"

"You said you haven't made any definitive plans, but Ambrose tells me you're thinking of selling the house."

"When did he tell you that?" Arden asked with a frown. She didn't like the idea of her grandmother's attorney repeating a conversation that Arden had considered private.

"Don't blame Ambrose. He let it slip in passing. It's none of my business, of course, but I would hate to see you sell. This house has been in the Berdeaux family for generations."

Was that a hint of bitterness in her uncle's voice? He would have every right to resent her inheritance. He was Evelyn's only living offspring. Why she hadn't left the property to him, Arden could only guess. In the not-too-distant future, her uncle would be the soul beneficiary of Clement Mayfair's estate, which would dwarf the worth of Berdeaux Place.

She rested her hand on one of the wooden tables. "It's not like I want to sell. Though I can't see myself living here. The upkeep on a place like this is financially and emotionally draining. I don't want to be tied to a house for the rest of my life."

"I understand. Still, it would be nice to keep it in the family. Perhaps I could have a word with Father. He's always had an interest in historic properties and a keen eye for real estate. And I imagine the idea of Evelyn rolling over in her grave would have some appeal."

Hardly a convincing argument, Arden thought in distaste.

"A word of warning, though. Keep everything close to the vest. Father is a master at sniffing out weakness."

Arden detested the idea of her grandmother's beloved Berdeaux Place being used as a final weapon against her. She'd have Ambrose Foucault put out feelers in other directions, although she was no longer certain she could trust his discretion. Maybe it was time to look for a new attorney.

She glanced at her uncle. "Please don't say anything to anyone just yet. As I said, my plans are still up in the air."

"Mum's the word, then. I should get going. I'm sure you'd like to get settled."

"It's been a long day," she said.

"Don't forget about the blooming party. And do stop by the studio when you get a chance. I'll give you the grand tour."

"Thank you. I would like that."

"You should probably also know that the Mayor's Ball is coming up. It's being held at Mayfair House this year, all proceeds to go to the construction of a new arboretum. You know how political those things are. Everything revolves around optics. If Father gets wind that you're home, he'll expect an appearance."

"Balls are not really my thing," Arden said with a shrug. She could hardly imagine Clement Mayfair hosting an intimate dinner, much less a grand ball, but as her uncle said, those things were political. She doubted her grandfather had agreed to throw open his doors and his wallet without getting something very valuable in return.

"He can be relentless when he wants something," her uncle cautioned. "It's never a good idea to cross him."

Arden lifted her chin. "I'm pretty stubborn, too. I guess that's the Mayfair gene."

Calvin's expression froze for an instant before a smile flitted. "Yes, we are a hardheaded lot. Maybe Father will have finally met his match in you. At any rate, your presence at the ball would certainly make things more interesting."

They stepped out of the steamy greenhouse into the cool evening air. He turned to her on the shadowy pathway. "Whether you come to the ball or not, Arden, I'm glad you're home. It's good to have someone in the house again."

"It's good to be here." *For now.*

"Good night, Niece."

"Good night, Uncle."

He strode down the flagstones toward the gate, pausing at the entrance to pluck a magnolia petal from a branch that draped over the wall. Lifting the blossom to his nose, he tilted his head to the moon as he closed his eyes and savored the fragrance.

Then he dropped the flower to the ground and walked through the gate without a backward glance.

Chapter Four

Reid pulled his car to the rear of the house and cut the engine. The bulb at the top of the back stairs was out. He'd been meaning to replace it, and now he decided that adding a couple of floodlights and cameras at the corners of the house might not be a bad idea. The neighborhood was normally a safe place, but a murder half a block from where he sat tended to make one re-evaluate security. He scanned the shadows at the back of the house before he got out of the car. Then he stood for a moment listening to the night.

Somewhere down the block, two tomcats sized each other up, the guttural yowls unnerving in the dark. He was on edge tonight. He rubbed a hand over his tired eyes, feeling weary from too little sleep and too many conflicting emotions. Seeing Arden had affected him far more deeply than he cared to admit. Maybe that was why he'd remained on the veranda after Evelyn Mayfair's funeral rather than going inside to offer Arden his condolences. He'd sensed even then that a face-to-face would awaken all those old memories.

Too late now to put that genie back in the bottle.

Already he could feel himself tumbling down the rabbit hole of their past.

He should have left well enough alone. There was no real reason she'd needed to hear about that magnolia blossom from him. She wasn't a little girl anymore. She could take care of herself. Truth be told, she'd never needed his protection, but there was a time when Reid had liked to think that she did.

Okay, so, big mistake. Miscalculated his feelings. Now he would have to make sure that he stayed on guard, stayed on his side of town, but why did she have to be one of those women who grew more attractive and interesting as she settled into her thirties? More desirable as the years went by with her sunlit hair and secretive smile?

A part of Reid wanted nothing more than to pick back up where they'd left off, while another part—the more distant and less-listened-to part—reminded him of the hurt she'd once inflicted. Maybe that assessment was overblown and unfair, but she'd turned her back on him when he needed her the most. When he'd been drowning in pain and confusion and desperately needed a lifeline. That she had been just as hurt and confused did little to soften the betrayal.

That was all water under the bridge. Reid had made peace with their estrangement years ago. He hadn't exactly been pining away. He'd sowed his wild oats and then some. No regrets. Still, no matter how much he wished otherwise, her homecoming wasn't something he could take in stride.

The back of his neck prickled as he scoured his surroundings. An indefinable worry blew a chill wind across his nerve endings, and he frowned as he tried to clear the cobwebs from his memory. Arden's return wasn't the only thing that had thrown him off his game tonight. The proximity of the murder disturbed him on a level that he didn't yet understand.

He'd come home last night, having called a cab from the bar where he'd spent the evening with friends. Vaguely he remembered paying the driver and watching the taillights disappear around the corner. As the sound of the engine faded, he'd heard the tom-cats fighting. Or had the sound been something else entirely?

He told himself he'd been sober enough to discern caterwauling felines from a human scream. But he couldn't shake the feeling that he'd seen something, heard something that had gotten lost in his muddled dreams.

He thought about walking down to the alley where the body had been found to see if anything jarred loose. He discarded the notion at once. The entrance was still cordoned off, and, for all he knew, the cops might have the street staked out in hopes the killer would return to the scene of the crime. Best not to get involved. He had enough on his plate at the moment. This was make-or-break time for the new firm, and he couldn't afford to get sidetracked by a murder or by Arden Mayfair or by an ex-con with an ax to grind against his family. *Keep your head down and stay focused.*

After locking the car door with the key fob, he climbed the back stairs and let himself into the apartment, flipping on lights as he walked through the rooms. The house was old and creaky, his living quarters in bad need of remodeling. But for now the space suited his needs. He didn't mind the peeling paint or the sagging doors or even the ceiling stains from a leaky roof. What he cared about were the long windows that let in plenty of natural light and the oak floors that had been worn to a beautiful patina. The house on Logan Street felt more like home to Reid than his sleek waterfront condo ever had. He'd never liked that place or the position at Sutton & Associates that had paid for it.

He poured himself a drink and then leaned against the counter to glance through the paper. The murder received only a scant mention. The victim's name was still being withheld, along with any details about the crime scene. Nothing about the magnolia blossom or any suspects. Nothing at all to explain that warning tingle at the back of Reid's neck.

He scanned the rest of the paper as he finished his whiskey and then poured another, telling himself he needed to relax, just needed to take the edge off that meeting with Arden. He still had a bit of a hangover from the night before so hair of the dog and all that. Booze had flowed freely at Sutton & Associates. The competitive nature of the firm had worn on the associates and junior partners, and Reid, like the others, had fallen into the habit of happy hour cocktails with clients and colleagues, wine with dinner, liqueur with coffee and then a nightcap to finish off the evening. Sometimes two or three nightcaps just so he could shut down and get to sleep.

Now that he was out of the pressure cooker environment of his father's firm, he needed to start taking better care of himself. Lay off the hooch. Hit the gym. Add a few miles to his morning run. Get back in shape mentally and physically. Turn over a new leaf, so to speak.

Resolved for at least the rest of the evening, he poured the remainder of his drink down the sink and then stuffed the newspaper in the trash can. Out of sight, out of mind.

It was too early to turn in so he went out to the balcony to enjoy the evening breeze. The house was built in the Charleston style—narrow and deep with the windows and balconies overlooking the side garden. If he turned his chair just so, he could glimpse the street through the lush vegetation. A ceiling fan whirled sluggishly overhead, stirring the scent of jasmine from his neighbor's fence. He propped his feet on the rail and clasped his hands behind his head.

This had become his favorite spot. Hidden from view, he could sit out in the cooling air and watch the comings and goings in the neighborhood while his mind wound down from the daily grind. Not that his schedule was all that packed these days, but he'd just taken on a couple of promising cases, and the stress of any new venture took a toll.

He'd been rocking gently as he let his mind drift, but now he stopped the motion and sat up straight as he listened to the night. The tomcats had long since called a truce and moved on. There was no traffic to speak of, no music or laughter from any of the nearby houses. Everything had gone deadly still. It was as if something dark had crept once more into the neighborhood. A shadowy menace that prowled the streets, luring young women into alleyways and leaving the kiss of death upon their lips.

Or white magnolia blossoms beside their dead bodies.

Reid chided himself for letting his imagination get the better of him. But the longer he stared into the darkness, the more certain he became that his house was being watched. Across the street, someone hunkered in the shadows.

It's nothing. Just a tree or a bush. No one is there.

But he was already up, leaning far over the balcony railing to peer through the oak leaves, zeroing in on a dark figure that didn't belong in the neighborhood.

The silhouette took on definition. Slumped shoulders. Tilted head. Reid could imagine the sneer.

Dave Brody.

Keeping to the shadows, Reid slipped back into the apartment, and then raced down the stairs and out the front door. But Brody had vanished by the time he crossed the street.

Probably not a good idea to go traipsing about his neighbor's yard, Reid decided. Good way to get shot. Instead, he circled the block, eyeing fences and garden gates until he found himself back on his street, standing at the alleyway where the young woman's body had been found early that morning. Police tape barricaded the entrance, but no one was about. No one that he could detect.

He lifted his gaze, searching along the buildings

that walled in the alley. Apartment windows looked down on the narrow street. Someone must have seen something, *heard* something. Had the police done a thorough job canvassing the area? Were they even now zeroing in on a suspect?

Reid turned to scour the street behind him, and he cocked his ear to the night sounds. The screech of a gate hinge. The scratch of a tree limb against glass. Somewhere at the back of the alley, a foot connected with an empty can. Or was that just the wind?

The sound jarred Reid and he told himself to go home. Leave the investigation to the police. He would be a fool to breach the police barricade and an even bigger idiot to pursue Dave Brody down a dark, deserted alley.

But when had he ever taken the prudent way out?

Ducking under the tape, he paused once more to glance over his shoulder. He could just make out his house through the lush foliage. He hadn't taken the time to lock up on his way out. If he was bound and determined to do this, he needed to be quick about it. For all he knew, Dave Brody could already be inside his house, hiding in a closet or underneath the bed.

Disturbing thought. Chilling image.

Almost as unnerving as exploring the scene of a violent murder.

He shook off his disquiet as he entered the alley, hugging the side of the building to avoid the glow from the streetlights. He came upon the bloodstains. There were a lot of them. Whoever the young woman had been, she'd met with a violent end.

Crouching beside the stains, he lifted his gaze to the buildings. The night was very still except for the quick dart of a shadow on one the balconies. Reid's pulse quickened as he strained to make out a silhouette. No one was there. Just his imagination.

He rubbed the gooseflesh at the back of his neck as he scoured his surroundings. A dog barked from behind a garden gate, and a fluffy yellow cat eyed him from atop a brick wall before leaping headlong into darkness. Night creatures stirred. Bats circled overhead. And somewhere in the alley, a two-legged predator watched from the shadows.

"Evening, Counselor," a voice drawled.

It took everything Reid had not to react to that whiny twang. Instead, he rose slowly, peering back into the alley as he said in a matter-of-fact tone, "That you, Brody?" As Reid's eyes adjusted to the gloom, the man's form took shape. He lounged against the wall of the building, one foot propped against the brick facade as he regarded Reid in the filtered moonlight. Reid couldn't see his features clearly, but he had no trouble imagining the tattoos, the buzzed head, the perpetual smirk. He hardened his voice. "What the hell are you doing back there?"

"I could ask you the same thing. Me? I'm just enjoying the night air while I check out the neighborhood. I always liked this area. Quiet streets. Friendly people. Maybe I should start looking for a place around here. Put down some roots. What you think about that?"

Having Dave Brody for a neighbor was the last thing Reid wanted to contemplate. And the irony of waxing poetically about the quiet streets while standing at the scene of a brutal murder seemed particularly creepy, but Reid knew better than to allow the man to goad him. "I saw you watching my house just now. You weren't out for a stroll. You were hiding in the bushes staring up at my balcony."

Brody turned his head and spit into the alley. "If I meant to hide, you wouldn't have seen me. I did tell you I aimed to keep an eye on you, didn't I?"

Reid clenched and unclenched his fists as he worked to keep his voice even. "We have more stringent stalker laws these days. You cross a line, I'll have your hide back in jail."

He could hear the amusement in Brody's voice. "I'm not too worried about that, Counselor. See, I had a lot of time on my hands in prison. Did a lot of reading. I know my rights and I know the law. I won't be crossing any lines. Just nudging up against them a little."

"You already crossed a police barricade. I could call the cops on you right now."

"But then you'd have to turn yourself in, and I don't think you want to get all jammed up with the Charleston PD right now."

Reid scowled. "What's that supposed to mean?"

Brody's gaze sliced through the darkness. "A good detective might start to wonder what *you're* doing in this alley, standing in the exact spot where a woman was stabbed last night. A good detective might start to dig a little deeper and find out you have a connection to the victim."

Reid's heart jumped in spite of himself. "Nothing

about the victim has been released to the public. No name, no description, no cause of death. There's no way you could know anything about her unless you—"

"I didn't lay a hand on her. Didn't have to. I just happened to be at the right place at the right time." Brody pushed himself away from the wall and came toward Reid. Despite the heat, he wore steel-toed work boots and an army jacket with crude lettering down the sleeves. It was dark in the alley, but enough light filtered in to emphasize the spiderweb tattoo on his neck and the three dots at the corner of his right eye. Common enough prison ink, but the images seemed even more ominous on Brody.

"Don't come any closer," Reid warned.

Brody laughed, displaying unnaturally white teeth in the moonlight. "See, I was in a bar on Upper King Street last night. Yeah, *that* bar. I saw you and your friends having a grand old time, not a care in the world. You were attracting plenty of female action, too, the way you were throwing around all that money. One gal in particular seemed mighty taken with you, Counselor. Kept trying to cozy up to you at the bar, touching your arm, whispering sweet nothings in your ear. She even passed you a note. Don't tell me you don't remember her. About yay-high, bleached blond hair?"

Something niggled at the back of Reid's mind. Although he tried to swat it away, a nebulous worry kept creeping back into his consciousness. "There were a lot of people in that bar last night. I didn't see you, though."

"Like I said, you won't see me unless I want to be

seen. I found myself a quiet corner just so I could take it all in." Brody reached inside his jacket and Reid reflexively stepped back. "Relax. I'm just trying to help jar your memory." He flung a photograph in the air and Reid flinched. The snapshot hung on the breeze for a moment before fluttering to the ground at Reid's feet. "Pick it up."

Reluctantly, Reid retrieved the picture, positioning himself so that he could use the light on his phone while keeping Brody in his periphery. He could make out a few faces in the photograph. His own, some of his friends. A woman he'd never seen before stood gazing up at him at the bar. Reid didn't recognize her, had only a hazy memory of someone coming onto him as he waited for a drink.

"Now do you remember?" Brody pressed.

"Who is she?"

"Who *was* she, you mean."

Dread rolled around in Reid's stomach as he glanced up. "What did you do?"

"I told you, I didn't lay a hand on her. See, I was out for a walk this morning when a bunch of police cars go roaring by. A guy in my position tends to notice that sort of thing. So I walk down here to see if I can figure out what's what. Got a look at the body before they bagged her up. Imagine my surprise when I recognized the blonde from the bar, dead in an alley not even a block from your place. Pretty little thing, too, but nothing like that blonde you went to see earlier this evening. Now she's a real looker."

Reid's head came up. "You stay away from her.

Whatever your beef is with me, she has nothing to do with it. You go near her place again, you even so much as glance down her street, I will personally see you back behind bars or in your own body bag."

"Mighty big words for a guy who's spent his whole life riding his daddy's coattails." Brody wiped his mouth with the back of his hand. "But no call to get all riled up, Counselor. I don't have any interest in your girlfriend so long as you help me get what I want."

"And what is it you want, Brody?"

"Justice."

"That's rich coming from you. What makes you think I'd ever want to help the likes of you? You haven't exactly been the poster child for rehabilitation since you hit town."

"Well, that's all in the past. Things have changed since last night. Now I'm in a position to help you out, too, Counselor. I'm hoping we can come to an understanding that will be mutually beneficial. See, that gal didn't just slip you a note last night. She put something in your drink."

Reid stared at him blankly. "What?"

"You wake up with a headache this morning? Have trouble remembering what you did and who you did it with?"

Reid's mind reeled back to the bar, to the cab ride home, to the cats fighting in the alley. When he'd finally tumbled into bed, he'd slept the sleep of the dead, awakening that morning to the sound of sirens outside his window. He'd had a dry mouth, a splitting headache and the sense that things had happened he couldn't remember.

All that flitted through his head in the blink of an eye.

Outwardly he remained calm as he casually glanced back at the street, telling himself to get the hell out of that alley. Whatever game Brody was playing, Reid wanted no part of it. Still, he lingered.

He turned back to Brody, dipping his head slightly as he peered into the shadows. "You just happened to be in a bar taking photographs when someone drugged my drink. That sounds totally believable."

"I didn't just *happen* to be anywhere," Brody said. "I followed you to that bar. I told you, I aim to keep an eye on you. As for the blonde, I never saw her before last night. She could have been working alone for all I know. Slipped you a roofie so she could roll you in the alley. You looked like an easy enough mark. My guess, though, is that someone paid her. Now you think about that for a minute. A woman comes on to you in a crowded bar and then she's later found dead half a block from your house. If the police start asking questions, someone will likely remember seeing the two of you leave together."

"I left the bar alone," Reid said. "I caught a cab and came straight home."

"Maybe you did, maybe you didn't. People tend to remember all sorts of things when an idea is put in their head. It's called the power of suggestion. The point is, you were seen with a woman who later ended up dead.

If I was a betting man, I'd say someone is setting you up, Counselor."

Reid was getting queasier by the minute. He told himself again to end the conversation. *Go home. Forget Brody. He's working a con on you.* "How do I know you're not making all this up? Or that you weren't the one who drugged me?"

"Plenty more photographs where that came from, and they tell a story. Two stories really. The blonde getting all touchy-feely—those photographs make you at the very least a person of interest if not an outright suspect. But the photographs of her slipping you a Mickey kind of make you look like a victim. Kind of proves someone is trying to set you up. See how that works? One set convicts, the other set clears. Now if the police were to get their hands on the wrong set, they might show up at your place of business, put you in cuffs, read you your rights and make a great big spectacle out of a Sutton arrest. Don't think they wouldn't get a charge out of that."

Oh, they would. Reid could see the headlines now. A famous defense attorney's son hauled in for questioning in a brutal homicide.

"Course, then your old man gets to swoop in and save the day," Brody continued. "But imagine his surprise when the one person who can clear his only son turns out to be yours truly." He gave a low, ugly laugh.

"You've given this a lot of thought," Reid said.

"Nah. The script practically wrote itself last night."

Dread was no longer tumbling around in Reid's stomach. It had settled like a red-hot coal in the pit.

"You say you want justice, but what specifically do you want from me?"

"Now we're getting somewhere," Brody said with an appreciative nod. "You worked for your old man's firm up until a couple of months ago. You know where they keep the files, the pass codes, where they bury the bodies, so to speak. I want you to find out what they did with a witness that could have corroborated my alibi. Her name was Ginger Vreeland, but I doubt she goes by that name anymore. She disappeared the night before she was to take the witness stand on my behalf."

"Maybe she got cold feet and left town," Reid said. "It happens more often than you think."

"Not Ginger. She was hard as nails, but she was loyal. We grew up together. She wouldn't have turned her back on me unless someone made her an offer she couldn't refuse. I've tried to find her over the years, but none of her kin is talking. I even hired a PI, someone I knew in the joint. He said it was like she fell off the face of the earth. Now, you don't vanish without a trace in this day and age unless deep pockets have funded your disappearance."

"You think someone paid her off," Reid said. "Why would they do that?"

"Not someone. Boone Sutton."

Reid stared at the man for a moment. "If you think my father would have intentionally thrown a case, you know nothing about him. Winning is everything in his book. Guilt or innocence is a distant second."

"Oh, I know him all right," Brody said. "I've studied up on all his cases. I know him inside and out and, yeah, you're right. He wouldn't have thrown a case unless he had a personal reason for doing so."

"And you think you know what that personal reason is?"

"I have a pretty good idea. Ginger was a working girl. The old-school type who kept track of her johns and their peculiarities in a little black book. If Boone Sutton's name was in that book, he might have been afraid of what she'd let slip on the witness stand. You say winning is everything to your daddy? I'd say reputation is right up there."

Reid wanted to deny the accusation, but he couldn't help thinking of all those nights his father never made it home. All the screaming matches between his parents that had eventually settled into contempt and then indifference. Their marriage had been one only in name for as long as Reid could remember. It was certainly possible his father had had a relationship with this Ginger Vreeland. If anyone could have helped her disappear without a trace it was Boone Sutton. He had contacts everywhere.

"There's no guarantee that Miss Vreeland's testimony would have cleared you," he said. "The evidence against you was overwhelming and the DA would have done everything in his power to discredit her as a witness. The outcome would probably have been the same."

Brody was quiet for a moment, and then he said with barely controlled rage, "That's not the point, Counselor. The point is, I deserved a fair hearing. I deserved an attorney who didn't sell me down the river. My rights should have been protected the same as anyone else's."

Reid steadied his voice. "In theory, I agree with you, but I don't know what you think I can do. How do you expect me to find someone who disappeared a decade ago when this person likely doesn't want to be found? I no longer work for my father. We barely even speak. The day I got fired, they took away my keys and changed the passwords and security codes after they escorted me out of the building. Even if I could manage to finagle my way through the front door, I wouldn't get near a computer, much less the file room."

Brody shrugged. "You'll figure something out. I'd start with your old man's home office. He's careful, but he's old-school like Ginger. He likes records. A paper trail even if it incriminates. You've got a lot riding on this, Counselor, so don't you go trying to sell me down the river, too."

"This is insane," Reid muttered.

"It's a little crazy, but play your cards right and we can both get what we want. Don't tell me you wouldn't like to take your old man down a peg or two. Think about it. You have until morning to give me your answer. Best you keep that photograph for incentive."

Reid glanced down at the dead woman's face.

"If I were you," Brody drawled, "I'd get back on home and find that gal's note before someone else does."

Chapter Five

It was after nine by the time Reid dragged himself downstairs the next morning. He hated getting such a late start. Made him feel as if he'd already wasted half his day. His only excuse was that he'd had a rough night. He'd gone home from the confrontation with Dave Brody and torn his house apart searching for the note the dead woman had allegedly slipped him in the bar. Then he'd poured himself a drink and searched again.

One drink had turned into a double and the next thing he knew, he'd been sprawled across his bed with a pillow over his head to drown out the street noises. He got up at some point to check the doors, drank a bottle of water, showered and then dropped back into bed. Sunlight streaming across his face had awakened him the second time. He drank more water, went for a run and then, after another shower, some ibuprofen and two cups of black coffee, he was finally starting to feel human again.

He'd just finished cleaning up the kitchen when a sharp rap sounded at the front door. He hadn't opened up the office yet, so he took a quick glance through the blinds. A tall man with a detective shield clipped to his belt stood on the front porch. His slicked-back hair and hawkish nose gave him an ominous air as he rested his hands on his hips, parting his suit jacket so that Reid could glimpse the shoulder holster beneath.

He turned the dead bolt and drew back the door. "Can I help you?"

The detective pointed to the plaque attached to the wall, which read Sutton Law Group. Then he glanced at Reid. "You Sutton?"

"Yes, I'm Reid Sutton. How can I help you?"

"I'm Detective Graham with the Charleston PD." He flashed his credentials. "I'm investigating a homicide that occurred in the area night before last."

"I heard about that." Reid kept his tone one of mild concern while, on the inside, he braced himself. Had Brody turned over the photographs to the authorities already?

After searching every square inch of the house, Reid had convinced himself the man had made up the whole thing. Brody had no other photographs; nor had he witnessed anyone drugging Reid's drink. No one was setting him up unless it was Brody himself.

But what if he was wrong? Reid found himself in a tricky situation, and on the slim chance that Brody could do real harm, he had to watch his step. He was an officer of the court and he believed absolutely in the rule of law. He didn't want to mislead, much less out-right lie to a police detective, but he also didn't want to volunteer unnecessary information. The less said, the better. Inviting scrutiny was never a good idea.

"Do you mind if I ask you a few questions?"

Reid nodded. "Whatever I can do to help, Detective."

"Can we talk inside? It's a real scorcher out here today."

"Sure. Come in." Reid pushed back the door to allow the detective to enter.

Graham stepped across the threshold and moved into the small foyer, glancing into what had once been the front parlor but now served as the reception area. On the other side of the entrance, the once formal dining room was now Reid's office, every inch of workable space piled high with file folders, contracts and briefs.

"Excuse the chaos," he said as he closed the front door. "I'm still getting settled."

"Just move in?"

"I've been here a couple of months."

The detective's gaze climbed the stairs. "What's up there?"

"My apartment."

"Just you here?"

"For the time being."

"Not much of a law group."

"Not yet, but I have big plans."

"I'm sure you do." Graham propped his hand on the banister as he scoured his surroundings. "Nice place."

"Thanks."

"An old house like this can be a real money pit, but the renovated buildings in the area are going for a mint. Good investment potential."

Reid could practically see dollar signs flashing in the detective's eyes. "Time will tell, I guess."

Graham dropped his hand to his side and turned with an apologetic smile. "Sorry. My wife's in real estate. I can't help noticing these things."

Reid brushed past him and stepped into his office. "Can I get you something to drink? Water, coffee…?"

"Water would be great if it's not too much trouble."

"No trouble." Reid walked back into the kitchen, where he grabbed a bottle of water from the fridge. When he returned to his office, Graham stood at one of the bookshelves perusing the contents. Reid placed the water bottle on the edge of his desk and then went around to take his seat, purposely drawing the detective away from any potential hiding spots he may have missed in his search for that note.

Graham took a seat across from Reid and uncapped the bottle. "I don't mean to stare, but you look familiar. Have we met? I'm not so good with names, but I rarely forget a face."

"It's possible," Reid said with a shrug. "Except for law school and college, I've lived in Charleston my whole life. I've practiced law here for the past five."

"You wouldn't be related to Boone Sutton, by any chance?"

Something in the detective's voice put Reid on guard. "He's my father."

Contempt flashed across the detective's face before he could hide his true feelings.

"I take it you're familiar with his work," Reid said.

"He's a legal legend in these parts. Not too popular at police headquarters, though."

"No, I don't imagine he would be. But you know what they say. No one likes defense attorneys until they need one."

"That is what they say." Graham glanced around the room. He still seemed fixated on the house. "Long way from Sutton & Associates on Broad Street. Talk about your prime real estate. That building must be two hundred years old if it's a day."

"It's a beautiful place," Reid agreed. "But I like it just fine where I am."

Graham canted his head as he regarded Reid across the desk. "Now I remember where we met."

"Oh?"

"I pulled you over once when I was still on patrol. You were maybe eighteen, nineteen years old, hauling ass down the I-26 in some fancy sports car. You failed the field sobriety test so I took you in. You're lucky you didn't kill someone that night."

"That was you?" Reid shifted uncomfortably. There were a lot of things in his past that he didn't much care to revisit. He'd gone through a reckless stage that could have ended badly for a lot of innocent people. Those days were long behind him, but some of his antics still haunted him.

"A kid like you needed a firm hand," Graham said. "But I guess your old man thought differently. He called in some favors and got you released without a mark on your record. And I was read the riot act for doing my job. Took me another five years to make detective because I pissed off some rich attorney with connections."

"I remember that night." Reid particularly recalled the part where he'd been used as a punching bag by a couple of thugs who'd joined him in the drunk tank. That experience had left a mark. "You had every right to take me in. I was a stupid kid back then and, yes, I am lucky I didn't kill someone. But if it makes you feel any better, I did learn my lesson. I don't get behind the wheel of a car if I've had so much as a glass of wine with dinner. I walk or I use a car service. So thank you. As for my father's interference, I can't do much about that except apologize. Your actions that night likely saved my life or someone else's. I was on a bad path."

The detective seemed unimpressed. "Guys like you always get second, third and fourth chances. Influence and money still go a long way in this town. Rules for me but not for thee, as they say. But if you really did turn over a new leaf, then more power to you." He sounded doubtful.

"I appreciate that." Reid sat back in his chair, discomfited by the detective's hostility. "I don't want to take up any more of your time. I'm sure you have a lot of people you need to talk to."

Graham took out his phone and glanced at the screen, leisurely scrolling through a series of text messages. He seemed in no hurry to get on with the interview.

"There hasn't been much about the case in the news," Reid prompted. "I understand the victim was a young female Caucasian."

Graham glanced up. "Where did you hear that?"

"People in the neighborhood talk," Reid said. "Did she live around here?"

"I think it would be best if I ask the questions."

"Of course. Force of habit." Reid smiled.

"Where were you on Sunday night?"

Right to the chase. Reid took a quick breath. "I went out to a bar to meet some friends. We were there for most of the evening. We had a few drinks, played some darts. It must have been just past midnight when I got home."

"You're sure about the time?"

"As sure as I can be. I didn't look at my watch or phone. The others weren't ready to leave so I hailed a cab. You can probably check the dispatcher's logs if you need the exact time…"

Graham didn't take notes. Reid wasn't sure if that was a good thing or not.

"You didn't see or hear anything unusual on the street?"

Reid paused. "I heard two tomcats fighting, but that's not unusual. They've been going at it for weeks."

Graham extracted a photo from his inside jacket pocket and slid it across the desk. "Do you recognize this woman?"

Reid braced himself yet again. He didn't want to give anything away with his reaction, but on the other hand, he had nothing to hide and he only had Brody's word for what had gone down in the bar. Best to be as straightforward as he could while taking care to pro-tect himself.

He picked up the photo, turning his chair slightly so that he could catch the morning light streaming through the blinds. He studied the dead woman's features. Blond hair, blue eyes. A wide smile. She was attractive, but not memorable. And yet there was something about her—

Was she the woman in Brody's photo? Hard to tell. His snapshot had caught her in profile in a dimly lit bar while this image was straight on.

Graham sat forward. "Do you recognize her?"

"I don't know her," Reid said definitively. "But there is something vaguely familiar about her. It's possible I've seen her before, especially if she lives in the neighborhood. Has her name been released yet?"

"Haley Cooper. Ring any bells?"

"No, I'm afraid not."

"She worked at one of the clothing shops on King Street. Roommate says she left their apartment around nine on Sunday night to meet up with a friend at a local bar. That's the last anyone heard of her until her body was found early Monday morning." The detective gave Reid a shrewd look. "You do any shopping on King Street recently? Maybe that's where you know her from."

"Or maybe she just has one of those faces," Reid said.

"That could be it." Graham tucked away the photograph. "I expect the chief will put out a full statement later today, but until her name is released to the public, I'd appreciate you keeping this conversation on the down low. If you think of anything…" He placed a business card on the desk.

"I'll call you," Reid said.

He got up to walk the detective out, trailing him onto the porch and then stopping short when he saw Arden lounging in one of the wicker chairs. She looked the embodiment of a Charleston summer morning in a yellow cotton dress and sandals. Her hair was pulled back in a loose bun and she wore only the barest hint of lipstick. The sprinkling of freckles across her nose gave her a youthful vibrancy that took Reid straight back to the old days. She looked at once wholesome and seductive, a suntanned temptation that smelled of raindrops and honeysuckle.

"What are you doing here?" he asked in surprise.

"Just dropping by to say hello. I hope I didn't come at a bad time." She rose and turned to the detective expectantly.

"Arden, this is Detective Graham. He's investigating a homicide in the neighborhood. Detective, this is Arden Mayfair, an old friend of mine."

She shot Reid a glance before turning back to Graham. "A homicide? That's alarming."

"Yes, ma'am, it is." The detective's attention lingered a shade too long on her slender form.

"Do you have any suspects?"

"That's not something I can discuss at the present."

"Of course. I should have realized that you're not allowed to talk about an ongoing investigation." She sounded contrite, but Reid detected a shrewd gleam at the back of her eyes. That was Arden. Wheels already turning ninety to nothing.

Graham continued to size her up. "Do you live in the area?"

"No, I live back that way." She gave a vague nod toward the tip of the peninsula. "I was just out for a stroll and decided to stop by and check out Reid's new place."

"You say your last name is Mayfair. As in Mayfair House on East Bay?"

"I don't live there, but Clement Mayfair is my grandfather. Do you know him?"

"Oh, sure. I was over there just last Sunday for dinner."

Arden blew off the detective's sarcasm with a smile and a shrug. "I find that hard to believe. I don't see any sign of frostbite."

"I beg your pardon?"

She exchanged another glance with Reid. "Mayfair House has a tendency to be bone cold even in the dead of summer."

"I see. Well, I'll have to take your word for that." Graham turned back to Reid. "You didn't mention the cab company you used."

"It was Green Taxi," Reid said. "I remember the driver's name. It was Louis."

"Shouldn't be too hard to track down. Maybe he saw something after he dropped you off."

"It's certainly possible."

Graham gave Arden a brisk nod. "Miss Mayfair."

"Detective."

She moved back beside Reid as they watched Graham depart. Once he was out of earshot, she said, "Not exactly the friendly sort, is he?"

"I get the distinct impression he doesn't like our kind."

"Our kind?"

"People who grew up South of Broad. Trust fund babies."

She wrinkled her nose. "Who does? Half the time, we can't even stand ourselves. Not that my trust fund is anything to write home about these days. Once work begins on Berdeaux Place, I'll be lucky to have two nickels to rub together."

"And I've been disowned so…"

They shared a knowing look before she turned back to the street. "What was he doing here anyway?"

"Graham? Just what I said. He's investigating a homicide in the area."

"*The* homicide?"

"Yes."

Her eyes widened. They looked very green in the morning light. "You never said anything last night about the murder being in your neighborhood."

"I didn't think it relevant."

She said incredulously, "Not relevant? Are you kidding me? After all our talk about the magnolia blossom found at the crime scene?"

Reid tried to downplay his omission. "I figured I'd already dropped enough bombshells on you for one night. I was going to tell you, just not right away."

Her gaze narrowed before she turned back to the street. "What did you tell the detective?"

"There wasn't much I could tell him. I don't know anything."

"Why did he come to see you?"

"He's talking to everyone on the street, apparently."

"Then why did he get in his car and drive off just now?"

"What is this, an inquisition? I don't know why he drove off. Maybe I was his last stop. I didn't ask for his schedule." Reid watched her for a moment as she watched the street. "Why are *you* here? Something tells me you didn't just drop by."

"No, I came for a reason," she admitted. "I have a proposition for you."

"A proposition? For me?" He ran fingers through his hair as he gave her a skeptical look. "The guy you couldn't get rid of fast enough last night?"

"That's not true. Things started out a bit rocky. You did catch me by surprise, after all. I wasn't expecting to see anyone in the garden, least of all you, and then you dropped your bombshells. Was I supposed to welcome you with open arms after that? I was a little preoccupied in case you didn't notice." She paused, slipping her hands into the pockets of her dress as she gave him a tentative smile. "The evening ended well enough, didn't it?"

He had been trying not to think about that kiss. The way she'd instantly parted her lips in response. The way, for just a split second, she'd melted into him. No one could melt like Arden. No one had ever made him feel as strong and protective and at the same time as vulnerable. "I guess that depends on one's perspective," he said.

Her smile faded and she grew tense. "I didn't come over here to pick a fight."

"Okay."

"I just…" She seemed at a loss as she closed her eyes and drew in a long breath. "Do you smell that?"

"You mean the jasmine? It's all over my neighbor's fence. Gets a little potent when the sun heats up."

"No, Reid. That's the scent of home."

Something in her voice—or maybe it was the dreamy look on her face—made it hard for him to keep up the pretense that her presence had no effect on him. He said almost sharply, "You didn't have jasmine in Atlanta?"

"Of course we did, but not like this. Not the kind of fragrance that sinks all the way down into your soul. There's no perfume in the world that can touch a Charleston summer morning." She hugged her arms around her middle as she drew in the scent. "I've missed this city. The gardens, the people, the history."

"Since when did you become so sentimental?"

"I get that way now and then. Comes with age, I guess. I even have my maudlin moments." She turned with her perfect Arden smile. "Would it be forward of me to admit that I missed you, too?"

Now it was Reid who had to take a deep breath. "Forward, no. Suspicious, yes. What are you up to, Arden?"

"Let's go inside and I'll tell you all about it."

He nodded and had started to turn back to the door

when he spotted a familiar figure across the street. Dave Brody stood on the sidewalk, one shoulder propped against a signpost as he picked at his nails with a pocketknife. He dipped his head when he caught Reid's eye and gave him an unctuous grin.

"Go on in," Reid said. "I'll be right back."

Arden followed him to the edge of the porch. "Where are you going?"

"Wait for me inside. This won't take a minute."

He hurried down the steps and across the street. This time Brody didn't run away. He waited with that same oily smile as Reid approached.

"Morning, Counselor. Mighty fine company you've got waiting for you over there on your front porch." He nodded in the direction of Reid's house and then lifted the hand with the knife to wave at Arden.

Reid glanced over his shoulder. Instead of going inside, she lingered on the porch, watching them from the shade. He could almost hear the wheels spinning inside her head. He turned back to Brody. "I told you last night, she's off-limits. That means don't wave at her. Don't talk about her. Don't so much as glance in her direction."

"Touchy, aren't we?" Brody pushed himself away from the post. "And I told you I have no interest in your girlfriend so long as you help me get what I want. I gave you the night to make your decision so here I am." He spread his arms wide as he moved toward Reid, displaying his ominous tattoos. "What's it going to be, Counselor?"

Reid frowned. "Not so fast. Did you have anything

to do with a police detective showing up at my door this morning?"

"No, I did not, but I'm flattered you think I have that kind of sway, considering my background and all. I couldn't help noticing the good detective—Graham, was it?—didn't look too happy when he drove away just now."

"How do you know his name?"

Brody gestured with the knife. The action seemed innocent enough, but Reid had no doubt it was meant as subtle intimidation. "He's been hanging around the neighborhood ever since the body was found. Surprised you didn't know that. Been preoccupied, have you?"

Reid wasn't buying any of it. "Are you sure you didn't say something to him? Maybe put a bug in his ear that caused him to come sniffing around my place?"

"Now that sounds downright paranoid. You're the lawyer. Don't it stand to reason he'd be talking to everyone in the neighborhood? Of course, it could be that word has already gotten out about your activities on the night in question. Or..." Brody shaded his eyes as he peered across the street. "Maybe someone else put that bug in the detective's ear. The same someone who's trying to set you up. Seems to me like you've made a powerful enemy in this town."

"And just who is this enemy?" Reid demanded. "Does he or she have a name?"

Brody dropped his hand to his side and shrugged. "How would I know? I'm just a guy who happened to be in the right place at the right time."

Reid thought about that for a moment. "Okay, let's

say I do have an enemy. If this person is already talking to the police, then how does it benefit me to help you?"

"A fair question, but you're forgetting something, aren't you? I have photographs that prove someone drugged you. I believe that's called exculpatory evidence? And then there's the matter of some video footage that happened to come my way."

Reid's pulse quickened even though he wasn't about to let Brody prod him into a reaction. "What footage?"

"I'll be happy to email you a copy for your edification, but for now a little preview will have to do." Brody took out his phone. "Amazing what they can do these days. Sure is a lot fancier than the one I had when I got sent up." He scrolled until he found what he wanted. Then he moved into the shade and held up the phone so that Reid could view the screen.

The video was grainy and greenish, like the feed from an outdoor security camera. Reid appeared in the frame and stood silhouetted at the entrance of the alley. Then he ducked under the crime scene tape and walked quickly to the spot where the body had been found, crouching beside the bloodstains as he glanced up to scour the windows and balconies that overlooked the alley. In actuality, he had been wondering if anyone had heard the victim's screams, but to the police, it might appear that he had come back to the scene of the crime to determine whether or not he'd been seen.

"I'm not a cop, but that looks mighty incriminating to me," Brody said.

Reid glanced up. "Where did you get this?"

"Like I said, it just happened to come my way and I'm not one to look a gift horse in the mouth."

"That video doesn't prove anything."

"Maybe, maybe not, but people get convicted on circumstantial evidence every day of the week. No one knows that better than me."

"Your situation was completely different," Reid said. "The evidence against you was overwhelming."

Brody looked as if he wanted to dispute that fact, but he let it pass with a shrug. "You're right. The video and those photographs won't send a guy like you to prison, but at the very least they can instigate an uncomfortable conversation with the cops. A perp walk is all it would take to scare off a sizable portion of your clientele. But there's no need for it to come to that. You help me find Ginger Vreeland and nobody sees any of this but us."

Reid glanced over his shoulder. Arden was still on the front porch waiting for him. He could imagine the questions going through her head. He nodded and gave a brief wave to let her know he'd be right there. "Even if I could find Ginger Vreeland after all these years, do you think I'd give you her name and address so that you can terrorize the poor woman?"

"You've got me all wrong, Counselor. I've got no beef with Ginger. She had to claw and scratch for everything she got just like I did. If somebody made her an offer she couldn't refuse, I can't fault her for taking it. I would have done the same thing in her place. All I want to know is who paid her to leave town and why. If it was Boone Sutton, then I want to know what she wrote in that little black book of hers every time he came calling. I bet, deep down, you'd like to know that, too."

"You'll never touch him," Reid warned.

"We'll have to see about that, won't we? Like I said last night, the best place to go looking is in his personal papers. A little birdie tells me that your mama spends a whole lot of time all by her lonesome in that fancy house on Water Street. I bet she'd dearly love a visit from her one and only son."

"Leave my mother out of this."

"That's up to you. If you can't or won't finish the job, then I'll have no recourse but to have a little chat with Mrs. Sutton. Find out what she knows about her husband's affairs. No pun intended." He went back to work on his nails with the pocketknife.

"All right, you win," Reid said. "I'll do what I can to find Ginger Vreeland, but she's been gone for ten years. The trail is ice-cold by now. I'll need some time."

"I'll give you till Friday. If you haven't made what I deem as sufficient headway, we'll have to reevaluate our arrangement. But fair warning, Counselor."

Reid waited.

Brody's gaze hardened as he moved out of the shade and stood peering across the street at Arden, running his thumb along the sharp edge of the knife blade. "I wouldn't go getting any ideas about trying to double-cross me. I have friends in low places. You know the kind I mean. Hardscrabble guys that would slit a man's throat—or a woman's—for not much more than the loose change in your pocket."

Chapter Six

"Who is that man?" Arden asked as Reid came up the porch steps.

"No one." He pushed past her and opened the front door.

"Didn't seem like no one to me. From where I stood, it appeared the two of you were in a pretty heated exchange."

"He's an ex-client," Reid said. "No one you need to worry about."

She gave him a long scrutiny. "Really? Because *you* sure look worried."

"Didn't you say you have a proposition for me?" He stepped back and motioned for her to enter, catching a whiff of her fragrance as she glided by him. The top note was honeysuckle, but he'd never been able to place the softer notes. He thought again of raindrops. And sunshine. Darkness and light. That was Arden. She'd always been a walking contradiction. An irresistible riddle with a killer smile.

Her timing was lousy, though. He considered making some excuse to send her on her way, but he didn't like the idea of her being out on the street even in broad daylight with Dave Brody lurking nearby. Smarter to keep her inside until Brody had had time to move on.

She hovered in the foyer, suspended in a sunbeam as her gaze traveled from the front parlor into his office and then up the stairs, just as Detective Graham had done before her.

"So this is your new place."

He checked across the street and glanced both ways before he closed the door. Despite Brody being nowhere in sight, Reid had a feeling he hadn't gone far. "What do you think?"

Arden shot him a look over her shoulder. "You want my honest opinion?"

"I would expect nothing less from you."

"You've got your work cut out for you. I would advise a gut job, but at the very least, the floors will need to be refinished and the windows replaced. The electrical and plumbing will undoubtedly cost a small fortune to bring up to code, and then you still have the less costly but time-consuming tasks of scraping wallpaper and painting drywall. But…" She turned with gleaming eyes. "I love it, Reid. I really do. The millwork is beautiful and the location is perfect. And all this natural light." She stepped into his office and went straight for one of the long windows that opened into the side garden. "This is my favorite style of architecture. I used to dream of owning a house like this. Do you remember? Berdeaux Place always seemed so oppressive to me."

"I remember."

Her gaze turned playful. "You always wanted something sleek and glamorous on the waterfront."

"I had that for a while. I discovered it didn't suit me at all."

She gave him an inquisitive look before turning back to the window. The yellow dress left her tanned back and shoulders bare. Reid had to tear his gaze from her slender form. Too many memories floated between them and his mind had a tendency to linger in dark places when he thought too much about the past. He needed a clear head to deal with Dave Brody. Needed to remain focused if he wanted to stay a step ahead of the police. And to think his life had been relatively uncomplicated just two short days ago.

"Do you want something to drink?" he asked. "I have some iced tea in the fridge."

"That sounds divine. The walk over was longer than I anticipated."

"You're not likely to cool off in here," he warned. "I've been meaning to get someone in to check the AC, but I'm spread a little thin these days." He picked up the detective's water bottle and carried it into the kitchen. Then he got down two tall glasses and poured the tea, taking his time until he had his mask back in place. "I have a couple of cases that have been consuming most of my time," he said in a conversational tone as he came back into his office and placed the drinks on his desk. Arden had already taken a seat, looking as comfortable as could be with her legs crossed and hands folded in her lap. One of the straps of her sundress had fallen down her arm. Reid had the urge to slide it back into place with his fingertip. Or to tug it all the way down with his teeth.

Yes, way to stay focused.

Arden seemed oblivious of his attention. Swiveling her chair around, she gestured to the file boxes strewn across the floor. "All that for just two cases?"

"One of them could be a class action."

"That's exciting." She leaned in to claim her glass and the strap slipped lower, revealing more than a hint of cleavage. Reid tried not to stare, but *damn*.

"What is it?"

"Nothing."

"You seem distracted."

"No, I'm all yours."

She looked doubtful. "I suppose we should get down to it then. I don't want to take up too much of your time."

He nodded. "Whenever you're ready."

She settled back against her chair. "My uncle Calvin was at Berdeaux Place last night. I ran into him in the garden. He said he'd been working in the greenhouse."

Reid frowned. "At night?"

"That's what I said, too. It just seemed odd. But considering his strained relationship with Grandmother, I would have been surprised to see him there at any hour."

"How did he get in?"

"He said he'd been letting himself in through the side gate so someone must have given him a key. Maybe Grandmother made arrangements before she died. I don't know. But, evidently, he's been coming by every evening to take care of Mother's cereus."

"Her what?"

Arden made a dismissive gesture with her hand. "It's a night-blooming cactus. Some call it a Queen of the Night. When it blooms, the scent is out of this world."

"You people and your flowers," Reid muttered.

"I know. We were all thwarted horticulturists, I think. Anyway, Calvin told me that Ambrose Foucault had mentioned my plans to sell Berdeaux Place. As you can imagine, I was pretty upset to learn that a conversation with my grandmother's attorney, one that I considered confidential, had been shared with my uncle."

Reid folded his arms on his desk. "Have you talked to Ambrose about it?"

"Not yet, but I intend to. As you can also imagine, Calvin wasn't too happy with the idea of my selling the house. He reminded me that Berdeaux Place has been in Grandmother's family for generations. I understand his position. Even though he never lived there, the house is his legacy, too. I don't want to be insensitive to his feelings, and at the same time—"

"Your grandmother left the property to you. You have the final decision."

"Exactly. And I don't take that responsibility lightly. Berdeaux Place was her pride and joy. Whatever I do, I want to make certain that the house and her memory are honored. But I have to be realistic about my prospects. Historic properties of that age and size come with a ton of legalities, so the pool of prospective buyers is limited. Grandmother left a contingency account and I still have money in the trust fund, but neither will last forever. I don't want to rush a decision, but I also can't afford to wait until I'm desperate and out of options."

"So put the place on the market as is," Reid suggested. "Get the ball rolling. You may be pleasantly surprised by the amount of interest the listing generates."

She idly twirled a loose strand of hair around her fingertip. "I've considered that, but now may not be the best time. I've reason to believe vultures are circling."

That got Reid's attention. He lifted a brow. "Are you worried about anyone in particular?"

"Yes." A shadow flitted through her eyes. She turned to stare out the front window as she gathered her thoughts. When she glanced back at Reid, the shadow had resettled into the hard gleam of determination. "Calvin told me that Grandfather might be interested in acquiring the house. He's always had an appreciation for historic properties."

"Well, there you go," Reid said. "Wouldn't that solve all your problems? The house stays in the family, and the burden is lifted from your shoulders."

"You're presuming his intentions are honorable, but I've never known Clement Mayfair to have an altruistic bone in his body. He's up to something. I just know it. His own son made the offhand comment that he might be interested in buying the house for no other reason than to imagine my grandmother rolling over in her grave."

"I'm sure Calvin was joking," Reid said.

"A joke based on an ugly truth," Arden insisted.

Reid canted his head as he studied her. "What are you really worried about?"

She took her time answering. "You'll think I'm paranoid, but I have a bad feeling that Grandfather is planning to take Berdeaux Place away from me somehow. He may even try to convince Calvin to challenge Grandmother's will. All I know for certain is that he has no sentimental interest in that house. He wants it out of pure spite."

"You really think he'd go to that much trouble and expense just to get back at a dead woman?"

"You have no idea the animosity that festered between them," Arden said. "They despised each other so much that they raised their children as strangers. Grandmother took my mother when she left and my uncle stayed behind with Grandfather. They barely ever saw each other even though they lived only blocks apart. I ask you, who does that kind of thing?"

"Relationships can be complicated, but that does seem a bit extreme." Reid thought about his mother spending so much time alone in the stately old mansion on Water Street. He felt a pang of guilt that he hadn't gone to see her in weeks, but they'd never been close. Her emotional distance had kept the two of them almost strangers. Why she stayed with Reid's father after so many years of contempt and neglect, he could only guess; undoubtedly, money played a role. She was a woman who appreciated her creature comforts. Now that Dave Brody had brought her into his machinations, Reid resolved to keep a closer eye on her.

He put that thought away for the time being and refocused on Arden. "You don't know what happened between them?"

Arden lifted a shoulder. "Grandmother would never talk about it, but I think it was something really bad. If Grandfather manages to get his hands on Berdeaux Place, I can only imagine the pleasure he would take in destroying it."

"You said yourself, there are rules and regulations that protect historic properties."

"He could burn it to the ground before anyone could stop him."

She'd worked herself into a state. Color tinged her cheeks and anger flared in her eyes, reminding Reid that Arden Mayfair had always been a woman of passion. In love, in anger, in hate. She gave it her all. Watching that fire burn out had pained him more than he wanted to remember.

"What can I do to help?" he asked quietly.

She glanced up gratefully. "If Ambrose can so easily be manipulated into revealing the details of our private conversation, then I can no longer trust him to have my best interests at heart. I'd like to hire you as my attorney."

That took him aback. "You want me to represent you?"

"Why not? Unless you don't want my business."

"It's not that. I think you'd be better served with

someone who has expertise in probate and real estate law."

She waved off his argument with another dismissive gesture. "How do I know another attorney couldn't be bought off by my grandfather? You're the only one I trust, Reid. I know you can't be bribed or intimidated. Not by Clement Mayfair, not by anyone. Quite the contrary, in fact."

She was just full of surprises today. He was the only one she trusted? A man she'd barely clapped eyes on in over a decade? A man whose heart she'd once broken and scattered to the wind without a hint of remorse?

Anger niggled and he gave it free rein for a moment even though he knew the emotion was irrational and unproductive. He sat in silence, observing her through his passive mask until he trusted himself to speak.

"I have to say, that's a pretty bold statement, Arden."

"It's true. I do trust you. I always have." She leaned in. "Will you do this for me? Will you take my case?"

"We don't know yet that there is a case. First things first, okay? I'll need to see a copy of your grandmother's will."

"I can get you one. Does this mean—"

"It means I'll take a look at the will. But the minute you start requesting documents from Ambrose, he'll know something is up."

"I know. I plan to talk to him as soon as I can arrange a meeting. I doubt he'll be upset. If anything, he'll probably be relieved not to be caught in the middle of a Mayfair war."

"If you're right about your grandfather's intentions,

the dispute could get ugly," Reid warned. "He has the resources to drag this out for years. Are you sure you don't want to sell him the house and be done with it?"

"Oh, I'm sure." She had that look on her face, the one that signaled to Reid she'd already dug in her heels. "Clement Mayfair needs to know that I'm not afraid of him."

Reid nodded. "Okay. I'll make some discreet calls and see if I can get wind of his plans."

"Thank you, Reid."

"Don't thank me yet. Let's just wait and see what happens." When she made no move to end the conversation, he shuffled a few papers on his desk. He would have liked to check the street, but she was already suspicious. The last thing he wanted was to put Dave Brody on her radar. "If that's all, I have a meeting to get to soon…"

She settled more deeply into her chair.

He sighed. "Something else on your mind, Arden?"

"I couldn't help noticing all the clutter here and in the other room. Books and files stacked every which way. It's the first thing you notice when you walk in the door and it hardly inspires confidence."

"That's blunt, but you're right. I haven't had a chance to put everything away yet. As I said, I'm spread a little thin these days."

She swiveled her chair back around to face him. "I could do it for you."

He stared at her blankly. "Why would you want to do that?"

"You need help and I need work."

He said in astonishment, "Are you asking me for a job?"

Her own mask slipped, revealing a rare vulnerability, but she tugged it back into place and lifted her chin. "Don't look so shocked. I'm not exactly a slacker, you know. I've been gainfully employed since college."

"My surprise has nothing to do with your work ethic."

She continued on as if he hadn't spoken. "What do you think I did at the museum all those years? I researched, appraised, processed and cataloged. Seems to me that is the kind of experience you need around here. I may not have a law degree, but I'm a fast learner and a hard worker. And you know you can trust me."

Did he know that? Fourteen years was a long time. People changed. Reid knew very little about her life in Atlanta or why she'd decided to come back to Charleston at this particular time. He had a feeling there was more to her story than settling her grandmother's estate.

But then, he was hardly in a position to cast stones. He hadn't been altogether forthcoming with her, either.

"Even if I thought this was a good idea, which I don't," he stressed "take a look around. Do you see a receptionist? A paralegal? Any associates? I haven't staffed up because I can't afford to. I used most of my cash to buy this house, and I promised myself I wouldn't dig any deeper until I was certain I could make a go of it on my own."

She tucked back the loose strand of hair as she gave him her most earnest, Arden appeal. "But wouldn't that be a lot easier with help? Just think about it, okay? I could file briefs, track down witnesses, do all the research and legwork that eats up so much your time. You don't even have to pay me at first. Maybe we can work something out with your legal fees. Give me a month, and I know I can prove myself."

"A month is a long time," he said.

"Two weeks, then, but you have to give me a fighting chance."

"I don't have to do anything."

The edge in his voice stopped her cold. Now she was the one who looked stunned. Rejection wasn't something Arden Mayfair would have ever gotten used to, he reckoned. The more things changed, the more they stayed the same.

"We were a good team once," she said. "Always a step ahead of everyone else, always in sync with each other. Together, we were formidable."

"That was a long time ago."

The furrows deepened as she gave him a long scrutiny. "Be honest, Reid. Are you letting our past color your decision?"

"I don't know what you mean."

"I'll be frank then. Are you still holding a grudge for the way I left town? What was all that business last night about airing our grievances? Were you just paying lip service to moving on?"

"We can move on without being in each other's face ten to twelve hours a day." He regretted the sharpness of his words the moment they left his mouth. He regretted even more the hurt that flashed in her eyes before she dropped her gaze to her hands.

"Point taken."

"Arden—"

"No, that's fine. It was a crazy idea. I mean, how could we ever work together after everything that happened between us, right?"

"Arden—"

"Don't say anything else. Please. Just let me walk out of here with as much dignity as I can muster." She rose. "I'll send over a copy of Grandmother's will as soon as I can make the arrangements. Unless you've changed your mind."

"No. I said I'd take a look and I will."

She turned toward the door.

"Wait." He winced inwardly, berating himself for succumbing to her emotional manipulation. He didn't think she was maliciously playing him, but she'd always known how to push his buttons.

She sat back down.

"We'll probably both live to regret this, but I may have something for you." He paused, deciding how far he wanted to take this. He could give her an errand or two, something that would occupy her time while he figured things out with Brody. Or he could just send her home where she would be protected behind the high walls of Berdeaux Place. Still, she was alone there and Reid had no way of knowing if the security system had been sufficiently updated. She might be safer here, with a police presence on the street and neighbors who were on guard for anyone suspicious.

"Reid?"

"Sorry. I was just thinking. I have outside meetings for the rest of the day. I won't be back here until late this afternoon, so you'll have the place to yourself. Take a look around, get acquainted with the house and help me figure out how I can best utilize the space. Long term, we can talk about tearing down walls and a possible expansion. For now, we work with what we've got. Upstairs is off-limits. That's my personal space and I don't want to be surrounded by work."

She nodded. "I can do that."

"You say you're good at research? See what you can do with this." He scribbled a name on a piece of paper and slid it across the desk to her.

She scanned the note. "Who is Ginger Vreeland?"

"Ten years ago my father represented a man named Dave Brody on a second-degree murder charge. The evidence against him was overwhelming, but Ginger Vreeland claimed she could corroborate Brody's alibi. She disappeared the night before she was to take the witness stand on his behalf. Brody was found guilty and sent to the state penitentiary."

Arden glanced up. "You suspected foul play?"

"No, more than likely someone bought her off."

"I don't understand. If this was your father's case, why are you getting involved?"

"Let's just say, Dave Brody has become my problem. He's out of prison and looking for answers."

"And you've agreed to represent him?"

"It's a complicated matter," Reid hedged as he opened a desk drawer and extracted a file folder.

"There's more where this came from, but the information inside is a good place to start. It includes notes
from the attorney that interviewed and prepped Ginger
Vreeland for her testimony. Read through the whole
thing and see if you can pick up any threads. It won't
be easy," he said. "Ten years is a long time and she's
likely changed her name at least once. She was a call
girl back then so there's no trail of W-2s to follow. I'm
not expecting miracles, but at the very least, you can
go through all the public databases in case something
may have slipped through the cracks."

Arden looked intrigued. "I'll need my laptop."

"You can use mine. I'll log you on as a guest." He
pushed back his chair and stood. "One more thing. As
soon as I leave here, make sure you lock the door behind me. Don't let anyone in that you don't know. In
fact, don't let anyone in but me."

She rose, too. "What about clients?"

"No one," he said firmly. "If anyone needs to get in
touch with me, they can leave a voice mail."

She followed him into the foyer. "What's going on,
Reid?"

He resisted the urge to put a hand on her arm. The
less physical contact the better for his sanity. "We can't
lose sight of what's happened, Arden. A woman's body
was found down the street from my house and a magnolia blossom was left at the crime scene. That connects
us both to the murder. Until the police make an arrest,
you need to be careful. We both do."

Something flashed in her eyes. A touch of fear,
Reid thought, but she looked no less dauntless or

determined. Her chin came up in that way he remembered so well. "I'll be careful. I'll lock the door behind you and I won't let anyone in until you get back. But you need to understand something, too." Her hazel eyes shimmered in golden sunlight. "No matter what happens, I'm not running away this time."

He drew a long breath and nodded. "That's what worries me the most."

Chapter Seven

Reid noticed the Mercedes as soon as he came out of the courthouse. Given the location, he might have assumed his father had tracked him down. The historical building that housed Sutton & Associates was just down the street from the intersection known as the Four Corners of Law at Broad and Meeting. But the long, sleek car was no longer Boone Sutton's style. He'd given up his limo and driver for a shiny red sports car on his sixtieth birthday. The way he tooled around town in his six-figure convertible was an embarrassing cliché, but that was his business. Reid had enough problems without worrying about his father's perpetual pursuit of his youth.

As he headed down the sidewalk, the driver got out and waited by the rear door.

"Mr. Sutton?"

"Yes." He tried to peer around the driver into the car, but the windows were too darkly tinted.

"Mr. Mayfair would like a word."

"Which Mr. Mayfair?"

"Mr. Clement Mayfair." The driver opened the back door. "Would you mind getting inside the car?"

Reid had never spoken more than a dozen words to Arden's grandfather. Truth be told, Clement Mayfair had intimidated Reid when he was younger, but he was a grown man now and his curiosity had been piqued. He nodded to the driver and climbed in.

The interior of the car smelled of new leather and a scent Reid couldn't pin down. Although the fragrance wasn't unpleasant, the mystery of it bothered him, like a memory that niggled. He drew in a subtle breath as he placed his briefcase at his feet and sank down into the buttery seat.

Clement Mayfair sat stone-faced and ramrod straight. Reid tried to recall the older man's age. He must surely be in his seventies, but time had worn easily on his trim frame. He had the same regal bearing, the same aristocratic profile that Reid remembered so well. His hair was naturally sparse and he wore it slicked back from a wide forehead. His face was suntanned, and his eyes behind wire-rimmed glasses were the same piercing blue that had once stupefied Reid into long, sullen silences.

Reid sat quietly now, only a bit apprehensive as he wondered what business the older man had with him.

"Mr. Mayfair," he finally said. "You wanted to see me, sir?"

"Do you mind if we drive? This is a very busy intersection and I don't like tying up traffic." His rich baritone had thinned only slightly with age.

Reid nodded. "I don't mind. But I have a meeting

in half an hour. I'll need to be back at the courthouse by then."

Clement Mayfair responded with a sharp rap on the glass partition. The driver pulled away from the curb and glided into traffic.

Reid watched the elegant neoclassical courthouse recede from his view with a strange, sinking sensation. He couldn't shake the notion that he had just made a serious mistake. Willingly entered the lion's den, so to speak.

He kept his voice neutral as he returned Mayfair's scrutiny. "How did you know where to find me?"

"You're an attorney. Call it an educated guess."

"That was some guess," Reid said.

The older man sat perfectly still, one hand on the armrest, the other on the seat between them. He wore a gold signet ring on his pinkie, which surprised Reid. Bespoke suit notwithstanding, Clement Mayfair didn't seem the type to appreciate embellishments.

He smiled, as if he had intuited Reid's assessment. "It might surprise you to know that I've kept track of you over the years."

"Why?" Reid asked bluntly.

"You were once important to my granddaughter. Therefore, you were of some consequence to me. Enough that I took an interest in your career. You were top of your class at Tulane Law. Passed the bar on your first try."

"I'm flattered you took the trouble," Reid said, though *flattered* was hardly the right word. Intrigued, yes, and certainly suspicious, especially after his con-

versation with Arden. He thought about her insistence
that her grandfather was up to something. Reid was
now inclined to agree and he braced himself for whatever attack or trickery might be forthcoming.

"You could have had your pick of any number of
top-tier law firms in the country," Mayfair said. "But
you came back to Charleston to work for your father's
firm. I've had dealings with Boone Sutton in the past.
I never liked or trusted the man."

"That makes two of us."

The blue eyes pinned him. "And yet you're very
much like him. Overconfident and self-indulgent."

"One man's opinion," Reid said with a careless
shrug.

Mayfair's gaze turned withering. "I suppose some
might find your glibness charming—I've always considered it a sign of a weak mind. You're educated and
reasonably intelligent, but you've never been a deep
thinker. You were never a match for my granddaughter."

Reid shrugged again. "On that we can agree."

"Then why did you go see her the moment she got
back into town?"

A warning bell sounded in Reid's head, reminding him to watch his step. A lion's den was no place
to let down one's guard. "Are you keeping track of
her…or me?"

"Charleston is still a small town in all ways that
matter. Word gets around."

"Let me guess," Reid said. "Calvin told you I'd been
by."

"I haven't spoken to my son in days. This isn't about

him. This is about my granddaughter." Clement Mayfair leaned in slightly. "You ruined her life once. Why not leave her alone?"

"That's an interesting perspective considering Arden is the one who left me."

"You got her pregnant when she was barely eighteen years old."

"*I* was barely eighteen years old."

"You were old enough to know that precautions should have been taken."

"We were not the first careless teenagers," Reid said.

"Still so cavalier."

Reid was silent for a moment. "How did you even know about the pregnancy? We didn't tell anyone."

"Did you really think I wouldn't find out?" His expression turned contemptuous. "I doubt my granddaughter would have agreed with me back then, but losing that baby was the best thing that could have happened to her."

Reid's fingers curled into tight fists as images flashed at the back of his mind. Arden's pale face against the hospital bed. Her hand clutching his as tears rolled down her cheeks.

"I can't speak for Arden, but I wouldn't have agreed with you then or now. And frankly, that's a pretty callous way of putting things."

"Doesn't make it any less true." Mayfair took off his glasses and methodically polished them with a handkerchief he had removed from his inner jacket pocket. His fingernails were cut very short and buffed to a subtle sheen. "Where do you think either of you would be if things had turned out differently? Would you have married her? Moved her with you to New Orleans and stuck her in some dismal campus apartment while you completed your degree? What about *her* education? *Her* ambitions?"

"This is the twenty-first century, in case you hadn't noticed. Women can do whatever they want."

"Don't fool yourself, young man. A teenager with a baby has limited options, even one with Arden's advantages. The marriage would never have lasted. You may not even have finished law school. I've little doubt that my granddaughter would have ended up raising the child alone."

"Well, we'll never know for certain, will we?" Reid turned to glance out the window as he pushed old memories back into their dark hiding places. In the close confines of the car, he caught yet another whiff of the mysterious fragrance, elusive and cloying. "I have to say, I'm curious about your sudden interest in Arden's well-being." He decided to go on the offensive. "You barely gave her the time of day when she was younger. Even when you invited her to dinner, she sometimes ended up eating alone."

"Arden told you this?"

"She told me everything."

The hand on the seat twitched as if Reid had struck a nerve. "I sometimes had to attend business even at the dinner hour. That was hardly my fault. A man in my position has obligations. But I'm not surprised Arden's recollection would cast me in a bad light. Her grandmother did everything in her power to poison the girl's mind against me just as she kept my own daughter from me years ago. Now that Evelyn is gone, I finally have the chance for a relationship with my granddaughter and I won't have you getting in the way."

Reid gave a humorless chuckle. "That you think I have influence over Arden shows how little you really know about her."

Clement Mayfair gave a grudging nod. "You have more fire than I remembered. Is that why you left your father's firm? The two of you butted heads? Well, I give you credit for that. It takes guts to strike out on your own, especially after being under Boone Sutton's thumb for so long. But I don't have to tell you the streets of Charleston are littered with failed attorneys."

Reid didn't trust the man's change in tactics. "I'm well aware of the risks."

"Then you must also know that in Charleston, it's more about whom you know than what you know. As for me, I never had much use for the elite, the so-called movers and shakers. I preferred building an empire on my own terms and, for the most part, I've been left alone. But you were raised in that environment. You know how the game is played. One word from the right person can make or break a career."

Reid said impatiently, "Is there a point to all this?"

Clement Mayfair put back on his glasses and tucked away the handkerchief. He blinked a few times as if bringing Reid back into focus. "I'm a quiet man who leads a quiet life. I prefer shadows to limelight. But don't mistake my low profile for impotence. A well-placed word from me will bring you more clients than you ever dared to imagine. Possibly even some of your father's accounts. A desirable feather in any son's cap. Or…" He leaned toward Reid, eyes gleaming behind the polished lenses. "I can see to it that your doors are permanently closed within six months."

Reid fought back another rush of anger. An emotional rejoinder would play right into Mayfair's hands. The older man was obviously trying to get a rise out of him. Trying to prove that he had all the power.

Reid smiled. "For all the interest you've apparently shown in me over the years, you seem to have missed the fact that I don't respond well to threats or ultimatums."

"I assure you, I've missed nothing, young man."

The car glided to a stop in front of the courthouse.

Reid reached for the door handle. "Thank you for the conversation. It's been illuminating."

Before he could exit the car, Clement Mayfair's hand clamped around his wrist. The man's grip was strong for his age. His fingers were long and bony, and Reid could have sworn he felt a chill where they made contact. He thought about Arden's claim that Mayfair House was bone-deep cold even in the dead of summer.

He resisted the urge to shake off Mayfair's hand. Instead, he lifted his gaze, refusing to back down. "Was there something else?"

"Stay away from my granddaughter."

Reid glanced at the man's hand on his arm and then looked up, straight into Clement Mayfair's glacial stare. "That's up to Arden."

The grip tightened a split second before he released

Reid. "Trust me when I tell you that you do not want me for an enemy."

There was a quality in his voice that sent a chill down Reid's backbone. "Seems as if I don't have much choice in the matter."

"I'm giving you fair warning. You've no idea the pain I can cause you." The older man's gaze deepened, and for a moment Reid saw something unpleasant in those icy pools, something that echoed the dark promise of his words.

Images swirled in Reid's head as he recalled Dave Brody's insistence that he had a powerful enemy in this city. He thought about the young woman from the bar who had ended up dead in the alley, her body riddled with stab wounds. Then he thought about Camille Mayfair, who had met the same fate, and Arden, only five years old and frozen in fear as her gaze locked onto the killer's through the summerhouse window.

It came to Reid in a flash, as his gaze locked onto Clement Mayfair's, that the elusive fragrance inside the car was magnolia. The scent seemed to emanate from the older man's clothing. Or did it come from the deep, dark depths of his soul?

That smell was surely a fantasy, Reid told himself. The sense of evil that suddenly permeated the car was nothing more than his imagination. Clement Mayfair was just a blustery old man. Powerful, yes, but not malevolent.

Even so, when the driver opened the door, Reid climbed out more shaken than he would have ever dared to admit.

ARDEN SPENT THE rest of the morning sketching floor plans as she went from room to room. She would bring a measuring tape the next day so that she could work to scale, but for now the exploration kept her highly entertained.

Curious about Reid's apartment, she took a peek upstairs. He'd been adamant that his private domain should remain off-limits, but only in so far as using it for an expanded work space. At least that's how Arden interpreted his instructions. Surely, he wouldn't mind if she had a look around. And, anyway, he wasn't here, so…

She climbed the stairs slowly, pausing at the top to glance around. The living area was sparsely furnished with a sleek sofa and an iconic leather lounger that had undoubtedly been transported from his modern apartment. A short hallway led back to the bedroom, a spacious and airy space with a high-coved ceiling and French doors that opened onto a balcony. A pair of old-fashioned rockers faced the street. Holdovers from the previous owner, Arden decided. She pictured Reid out there in the evenings, breeze in the trees, crickets serenading from the garden. She could see herself rocking beside him, head back, eyes closed as the night deepened around them.

Thinking about Reid in such an intimate setting evoked too many memories. He'd once been the most important person in her life. Her soul mate and lifeline. Sad to contemplate how far they'd drifted apart. Sadder still that pride and willfulness had kept her away for so long. She wondered what his reaction would be if he discovered the real reason she'd come back to Charleston, tail between her legs, looking to start anew from the unpleasantness she'd left behind in Atlanta. No use dwelling on bad memories. No sense conjuring up the pain and humiliation that had hung like a bad smell over her abrupt departure. She had a mission now. A purpose. No more spinning her wheels.

She closed the French doors and went back downstairs. Taking a seat behind Reid's desk, she set to work, scribbling notes on a yellow legal pad she'd found in one of the boxes before turning her attention to the name she'd been tasked to research. Ginger Vreeland.

Taking his suggestion, she read through the file, quickly the first time and then more slowly the second, making more notes on the same legal pad. The hours flew by, and before she knew it her stomach reminded her that she'd worked through lunchtime. She went into the kitchen to check the refrigerator, helping herself to the last container of blueberry yogurt before returning to her assignment.

Research could be tedious, and she knew enough to pause now and then to stretch her legs and work out the kinks in her neck and shoulders. She'd just settled back down from a brief respite when she heard someone at the back door. She assumed Reid had returned and barely gave the intrusion a second thought until she remembered he was supposed to be away until late that afternoon.

Rising slowly, she walked across the room to peer into the kitchen. She could see someone moving about on the porch through the glass panel in the door. The man was about the same height and size as Reid, but she knew instinctively it wasn't him even though she never got a look at his face.

Pressing against the wall, she had started to take another peek when she heard the scrape of a key in the lock. Then the door handle jiggled. Alarmed, Arden glanced around the office, wondering what she should do. Wait and confront the interloper? Let him know she was there before he got inside?

She did neither, opting to heed the little voice in her head that commanded her to hide. She had no idea who else would have a key to Reid's house, but she wasn't about to wait around and find out. Hadn't Reid warned her not to let anyone inside? Hadn't he reminded her that the proximity of his office and the magnolia blossom left at the crime scene connected them both to the murder? And to the murderer?

Hurrying across the office, Arden stepped into the foyer, taking another quick glance around. Slipping off her sandals, she hooked them over her finger as she ran quietly up the stairs, pausing on the landing to peer over the banister. She heard the back door close a split second before she retreated into Reid's apartment. She made for the bedroom, wincing as a floorboard creaked beneath her bare feet. After tiptoeing across the hardwood floor, she opened the closet door and dropped to her knees, pulling the door closed behind her. Then she scrambled into the corner, concealing herself as best she could with Reid's clothing.

The closet wasn't large. If the intruder wanted to find her he could do so without much effort, but Arden had been nearly silent in her escape. He hadn't heard her. He didn't know she was there. She kept telling herself that as she drew her knees to her chest, trying to make herself as small a target as possible. There could be any number of legitimate reasons someone would have a key to Reid's house. Maybe he'd given a spare to a repairman or a neighbor. Maybe he had a cleaning service that he'd neglected to tell her about. Maybe Reid himself had returned and she'd allowed panic to spur her imagination.

She kept telling herself all those things right up until the moment she heard slow, heavy footsteps on the stairs. The intruder approached the second floor with purpose. He knew she was there. Knew there was no escape.

Why hadn't she gone out the front door or even onto the balcony? Maybe she could have shimmied down a tree or a trellis. She wasn't afraid of heights. She could have even climbed up to the roof and waited him out.

She scooted toward the door, thinking she might still have time. She reached for the knob and then dropped her hand to her side. He was in the bedroom already. How had she missed the sound of his footsteps in the other room?

Holding her breath, she flattened her hands on the floor and pushed herself back into the corner, taking care not to disturb the hangers. She pulled her knees back up and waited in the dark.

He walked around the room, taking his time as he opened and closed drawers, checked the balcony and then moved back into the room. Arden clamped a hand over her mouth to silence her breathing. She couldn't see anything in the closet. Could barely detect his footsteps. Had he left already? Did she dare take a peek?

The closet door opened and a stream of light edged up against her. She shrank back, unable to see the intruder. She didn't dare part the clothes to get a look at his face, but she sensed him in the doorway. Waiting. Listening.

An image came to her of a woman's body in a dark alleyway, and of a figure—gloved and hooded—bending over her as he placed a magnolia blossom on the ground beside her. She could almost smell that scent. The headiness took her back to that summer twilight when she'd discovered her mother's lifeless body in the garden with the crimson kiss of death upon her lips. Arden thought of the killer watching her from the summerhouse window, leaving a pristine blossom on the steps as a warning that he would someday return for her.

Adrenaline pumped hard and fast through her veins. She smothered a scream as the wooden hangers clacked together. In another moment, he would part Reid's clothing and discover her cowering in the corner.

He rifled through a few items and then stepped back. A folded paper square fell to the floor. Arden could see it in a patch of sunlight. She didn't know if the note had come from one of Reid's pockets or if the intruder had dropped it. If he bent to pick it up, he would surely see her. He didn't pick it up. Instead, he kicked the note back into the closet, as if he didn't want it to be found. At least not right away.

The closet door closed. The footsteps receded across the bedroom floor, into the living room and then down the stairs. Arden lifted her head, turning her ear to the sound. She was almost certain she heard the back door close, but she waited for what seemed an eternity before she ventured from her hiding place.

She grabbed the note as she scrambled to her feet and all but lunged from the closet, drawing long breaths as she tried to calm her pounding heart. Then she slipped through the rooms, pausing at the top of the stairs to listen once more before slowly descending. She went through every room checking doors and windows, and only when she was satisfied that she was alone did she go back into Reid's office and open the folded note.

A woman's name and phone number were scrawled in flowery cursive across the paper and sealed with a vivid red lipstick print.

The crimson kiss of death.

Chapter Eight

Arden jumped when she heard footsteps on the front porch. She was seated at Reid's desk trying to concentrate on work, but now she leaped to her feet and hurried over to the window to glance out. She could see Reid through the sidelight. Before he had a chance to insert his key in the lock, she drew back the door, grabbed his arm and all but yanked him inside. She'd never been so relieved to see anyone.

"Hello to you, too," he quipped, and then he saw her face as she closed the door and turned the dead bolt. He tossed his jacket on the banister and removed his sunglasses. "Arden? What's going on?"

"Someone broke into your house after you left."

"What?" He took her arm. "Are you okay? Were you hurt?"

Even as shaken as she was, his concern still gratified her. "I'm fine. I wasn't touched. He never even saw me. When I realized it wasn't you, I went upstairs and hid."

"How did he get in?"

"He came in through the back door."

His hand tightened on her arm as he glanced past

her into the kitchen. Then his gaze shot back to her. "Are you sure you're okay?"

"I was scared and I'm still a little wobbly, but I'm fine."

He laid his sunglasses on the entrance table without ever releasing her. "When did all this happen?"

"A little while ago."

"Did you call the police?"

Arden hesitated. She hadn't called the police. She hadn't called anyone. The reason didn't matter at the moment. They would get to that later. "There wasn't time. It happened so quickly…"

He took both her arms and studied her intently as if he needed to prove to himself she wasn't injured. She inhaled sharply. She'd forgotten how dark his eyes were. A deep, rich brown with gold flecks that looked like tiny flares in the sunlight streaming in through the windows. He'd removed his tie and rolled up his shirtsleeves. He was very tanned, Arden noticed. She wondered if he still went to the beach on weekends. She wondered a lot of things about Reid's life, but now was not the appropriate time to ask questions or wallow in memories. An hour ago, she'd been certain an old killer had come to track her down. She could still picture his shadow across the closet floor, could still hear the sound of his breath as he stood in the doorway searching through Reid's clothes. Had he known she was there all along? Had he left her alone in order to prolong his sick game?

"Arden?"

She jumped. "I'm sorry. What did you say?"

Reid canted his head as if trying to figure something out. "Can you tell me what happened?"

She nodded. "I said someone broke in, but that's not entirely accurate. He had a key. He let himself in the back door, and he didn't seem at all worried about being caught. He must have seen you leave and thought the house was empty." She moved away from Reid's touch and turned to glance back out at the street. Everything looked normal, but she could imagine someone out there watching the house, perhaps plucking a magnolia blossom from a nearby tree as he vectored in on the window where she stood.

"Did you get a look at him?" Reid asked. "Can you describe him?"

"Not really. I only glimpsed him through the window. He seemed to be about your general height and build." She scoured a neighbor's yard before turning back to Reid. "Have you given a key to anyone lately? A repairman or a neighbor maybe?"

"I don't give out my keys." He spoke adamantly.

"Did you get the locks changed after you moved in?"

He winced. "I've been meaning to."

"*Reid.* That's the first thing you're supposed to do when you move into a new place."

"I know that, but I've been a little busy lately." Now he was the one who turned to glance out the window. He looked tense as he studied the street. They were both on edge. "This is my fault," he said. "I should never have left you here alone."

She scoffed at his reasoning. "Don't be ridiculous. You couldn't have known something like this would

happen. And you did caution me not to let anyone in.
That's why I hid. I kept thinking about what you said
earlier. We're both connected to that murder. If your
warning hadn't been fresh on my mind, I might have
confronted him. Who knows what would have happened then?"

"You've always been quick on your feet," Reid said.
"So you went upstairs to hide. Could you tell if anything was missing when you came back down?"

"I don't think he took anything. But he may have
left something."

Reid frowned at her obliqueness. "What do you
mean?"

"He went up to your apartment. By that time, I was
hiding in your closet and I couldn't see anything. I
heard him walking around in the bedroom, opening
dresser drawers and looking out on the balcony. When
he came over to the closet, I was certain he knew I was
in there. You can't imagine the things that went through
my head. I even thought I smelled magnolia..." She
rubbed a hand up and down the chill bumps on her
arm. "You must think I'm crazy."

He gave her a strange look. "Because you smelled
magnolia? No, I don't think you're crazy. Far from it.
What happened then?"

"He dropped a note on the floor. Or else it fell out
of one of your pockets. He kicked it to the back of the
closet as if he didn't want you to find it right away."

Reid had gone very still. Something flickered in his
eyes. "Do you have the note?"

She took it from her dress pocket and handed it to

him. He unfolded the paper and scanned the contents. Arden watched his expression. The look that came over his face frightened her more than the intruder.

"That's the dead woman's name, isn't it?" she asked quietly.

He glanced up from the note. "How did you know?"

"The police chief had a press conference earlier. I streamed it while I worked."

"Did he say anything about suspects? Or the magnolia blossom?"

"He was pretty vague. They're pursuing several leads, leaving no stone unturned and all that, but he didn't say a word about the magnolia blossom."

"They're still keeping that close to the vest," Reid said.

"Or else they have no idea of the significance."

"I think they know. They don't want to panic the public with premature talk of a copycat killer."

"Maybe," Arden said pensively. "I keep going back to my mother's murder. The magnolia blossom left on the summerhouse steps was all but forgotten because the crimson kiss of death soon became Finch's signature. You said yourself only a handful of people would understand the implication of a *white* magnolia blossom. You and I are two of them. My mother's killer is a third."

"I don't want to get sidetracked with a long conversation about Orson Lee Finch's guilt or innocence," Reid said. "Right now, we need to focus on our immediate situation."

"I agree. First things first. Why would someone break

into your home and leave that note? Did you know this woman?" Arden had expected an instant denial; instead, he dropped his gaze to the note, pausing for so long that her heart skipped a beat. "Reid?"

He glanced up. "I didn't know her, but it's possible I may have seen her on the night she was murdered."

Arden caught her breath. "When? Where? Why didn't you say anything?"

"Because I didn't know until last night. I'm still not certain it was her."

"Reid—"

He headed her off. "I'll tell you everything I know, but I need a drink first. It's been a long day."

Arden followed him into the kitchen. When he got a bottle of whiskey from one of the cabinets, she took it from him and poured the contents down the sink.

He didn't try to stop her, though his look was one of annoyance. "Why did you do that?"

"Because a drink is the last thing you need," she said firmly. "Until we figure out what's going on, we both need to keep a clear head."

He looked as if he wanted to argue, and then he shrugged. "Water, then."

She handed him a chilled bottle from the refrigerator. He took a long swig before recapping and setting it aside. "Let's go sit in my office. This could take a while."

Arden led the way this time, taking the position behind his desk where she had been working earlier. Reid didn't seem to notice or care. He plopped down in a chair across from her, his long legs sprawled in front of him as he braced his elbows on the armrests.

"Where should we start?" Arden asked.

"I'm still trying to figure out why you didn't call the police," he said.

"I told you. There wasn't time."

"I mean afterward. Why didn't you at least call me?"

"You said you had meetings all afternoon. I didn't want to leave a voice mail. I thought it better that I tell you in person. As for the police..." She paused. "How long have we known each other? Since we were four years old, right? Has there ever been a time when I couldn't read you like a book?"

He lifted a brow but kept silent.

"I knew the moment you came to Berdeaux Place last evening that you were keeping something from me. I felt it even stronger this morning. I didn't want to involve the police until I could figure out what you might be mixed up in."

Reid looked taken aback by her revelation. "You were trying to protect me?"

"Why does that surprise you? We've always had each other's back."

"Fourteen years, Arden."

"So?"

"That's a long time."

"Some things don't change, Reid." She tried not to think about the loneliness of those fourteen years. "My turn to ask the questions," she said briskly. "Who was that man on the street you talked to this morning?"

He answered without hesitation, as if he'd decided

it was pointless to keep things from her any longer. "Dave Brody."

"Your father's ex-client? What did he want?"

Reid sighed. "It's a long story—in a nutshell, he has a bone to pick about his defense. Ever since he got out of prison, he's been coming around making veiled threats. He watches the house, follows me when I leave. That sort of thing."

"But you weren't his attorney. Why is he harassing you?"

"He wants me to help prove that my father was responsible for Ginger Vreeland's disappearance."

Arden stared at him in shock. "Responsible...how? He doesn't think—"

"No, nothing like that. He thinks she was paid to leave town."

"That's still insane. Boone Sutton is one of the best defense attorneys in the state. Why would he get rid of his own witness?"

"Apparently, Ginger kept a little black book with all her clients' names and their preferences. Kinks. Whatever you want to call them. Brody is convinced my father was one of her clients. He was afraid of what might come out during her testimony so he arranged for her to disappear."

"But she was prepped for her testimony. Wouldn't he have known what she would say before he called her to the witness stand?"

"Witnesses have been known to fall apart under cross-examination," Reid said. "Plus, we don't know what went down between them before she left town.

Maybe she blackmailed him. Offered to keep quiet in exchange for money."

"Wow." Arden sat back against the chair. "I have to say, this is getting really interesting."

"I'm glad you're entertained."

"Don't tell me you're not. Boone Sutton and a prostitute? Wouldn't that set tongues to wagging!" A dozen questions bubbled, but Arden batted them away so that she could remain focused on the situation at hand. "What happens if we find Ginger Vreeland and her little black book? What does Brody plan to do with the contents?"

"My guess is, he's looking for a big payday. Barring that, he'll settle for my father's public humiliation."

"And you're helping him," Arden said. "So what does he have on you?"

"Are you sure you want to hear this?"

"Yes, I think I'd better."

He told her about the confrontation in the alley and Brody's claim that he had photographs from the bar. He told her about the note, the laced drink and the possibility that someone with a lot of power was setting him up for murder. Arden leaned forward, watching his expression as she hung on his every word.

By the time he finished, she was aghast. "This is unreal. Who would do such a thing?"

"I don't know."

"Are you sure Brody's not the one setting you up? Or maybe he's just making it all up to get you to help him."

"He showed me a photograph from the bar, so he's

not making everything up. As to the rest…" Reid shrugged. "I don't put anything past him."

"What are you going to do?"

"For the time being, try to keep a low profile." He massaged his temples with his fingertips.

"What did you tell the detective who came by here this morning?"

"Nothing of what I just told you."

"Why not? If someone is setting you up, the police need to know about it. At the very least, you should tell them about Brody's threats."

Reid dropped his hands back to the armrests. "You saw the way Detective Graham looked at us this morning. He didn't even bother to hide his contempt."

"He did have an attitude," Arden agreed.

"More than an attitude. He came to my front door with a chip on his shoulder. Turns out, our paths have crossed before. He arrested me several years back. Apparently, my father pulled strings to arrange for my release and have my record expunged. Then he made sure Graham wasn't promoted to detective for another five years."

Arden digested that for a moment. "Does your father have that kind of clout with the police department?"

"Yes. But if he interfered with anyone's career, it likely had more to do with my black eye and cracked ribs than it did with the initial arrest."

"Graham beat you up?"

"Not personally, no. Two thugs jumped me in the holding cell, and I'd be willing to bet Graham was behind the attack. I think he wanted to teach me a lesson.

Dear Reader,

IT'S A FACT: if you answer 4 quick questions, we'll send you 4 FREE REWARDS!

I'm not kidding you. As a leading publisher of women's fiction, we value your opinions... and your time. That's why we are prepared to **reward** you handsomely for completing our mini-survey. In fact, we have 4 Free Rewards for you, including 2 free books and 2 free gifts.

As you may have guessed, that's why our mini-survey is called **"4 for 4".** Answer 4 questions and get 4 Free Rewards. It's that simple!

Thank you for participating in our survey,

Pam Powers

Maybe he still does. The point is, if he gets a look at those photographs, he'll zero in on me to the exclusion of any other leads or suspects. If he goes to the bar and asks the right questions, someone may remember that they saw me leave with the victim. I didn't," he added quickly. "But Brody is right. The power of suggestion is a real thing. That's why eye-witness testimony can be so unreliable."

Arden shook her head. "I had no idea all this was going on. No wonder you looked like death warmed over when I got here this morning."

"Felt like it, too."

She said hesitantly, "This is a long shot, but you don't think your father could be behind this, do you? You said you were fired from Sutton & Associates. It must have been a serious falling-out if he also disowned you. Maybe this is *his* way of teaching you a lesson."

"Boone Sutton is a lot of things, but he's no murderer," Reid said.

"Maybe that girl wasn't supposed to die. Maybe Brody was just supposed to harass you so that you would be forced to return to the firm. But he took matters into his own hands because he has his own agenda."

"It's possible, of course, but I don't see my father getting into bed with a guy like Dave Brody. Not with their history."

"Their history is precisely why he would have thought of Brody in the first place. But leaving that aside, is there anyone else who would want to frame you? Do you have any other enemies that you know of?"

He scowled at the window as if he were deep in thought. "There may be someone," he said slowly. "You're not going to like hearing about it, though."

"I take it you don't mean Detective Graham."

Reid's gaze came back to hers. "Your grandfather was waiting for me when I came out of the courthouse earlier. He asked me to take a ride."

"What?" Arden could hardly comprehend such a thing. "Clement Mayfair asked you to take a ride? Why? What did he want?"

"He warned me to stay away from you."

"What?"

Reid nodded. "He thinks now that your grandmother is gone he can have a relationship with you. He doesn't want me standing in the way."

"He said that? I'm...speechless," Arden sputtered.

"I was pretty surprised myself," Reid said.

"Surprised doesn't even begin to cover it. That man...that *insufferable man*...has never once shown the slightest bit of interest in me, and now he's warning you to stay away from me?" She got up and paced to the window. "This just proves I'm right. He's up to something."

"I think so, too," Reid said. "Until we can figure out his agenda, you should stay away from him."

She marched back to the desk and plopped down. "Oh, no. I'm going over there tonight to give him a piece of my mind."

"Arden, don't do that."

"Who does he think he is? He can't bully my friends

and get away with it. He can't bully me. I won't let him."

"Calm down, okay? I understand how you feel but listen to me for a minute. Arden? Are you listening?"

She folded her arms. "What?"

"Clement Mayfair is a powerful man with unlimited resources. We have to be careful how we take him on. We have to keep our cool. He said I didn't want him for an enemy and I believe him."

She glanced at Reid in alarm. "Does this mean you don't want to take my case? Maybe you don't want me working here, either. I understand if you don't. I could walk out the door right now, no hard feelings."

"I didn't say any of that."

"I know, but I came here this morning and more or less forced myself on you."

A smile flitted. "I'm not sure I would put it quite that way."

"You know what I mean. I made it nearly impossible for you to say no to me. I'm giving you that chance now. Say the word, Reid."

He gave her an exasperated look. "Did you even hear what I said? We need to be careful how we take him on. *We*. Us. You and me."

"You don't have to do this."

He entwined his fingers beneath his chin as he gazed at her across the desk. "Weren't you the one who said we make a formidable pair?"

"Yes, but that was before I knew my grandfather had threatened you. You're trying to start your own firm. The last thing you need is Clement Mayfair making trouble for you. And you don't need to protect me. I can take care of myself."

The gold flecks in his eyes suddenly seemed on fire as his gaze intensified. "I told you before, old habits die hard."

"Fourteen years, Reid."

"Some things don't change."

ARDEN HAD A difficult time forgetting that look in Reid's eyes. She thought about it all the way home. She thought about it during an early, solitary dinner, and she was still thinking about those golden flecks when she drifted out to the garden. The sun had dipped below the treetops, but the air had not yet cooled. The breeze that blew through the palmettos was hot and sticky, making her wonder if a storm might be brewing somewhere off the coast.

She started down the walkway, taking note of what needed to be done to the gardens. She wouldn't linger long outside. Once the light started to fade, she would hurry back inside, lock the doors, set the alarm and curl up with a mindless TV program until she grew drowsy. For now, though, she still had plenty of light, and the exotic dome of the summerhouse beckoned.

As tempted as she was by memories, she couldn't bring herself to climb the steps and explore the shadowy interior. She diverted course just as she had last evening, finding herself once again at the greenhouse. She peered through the glass walls, letting her gaze travel along the empty tables and aisles. No one was about. She wondered if her uncle had already been by before she got home. He had been cordial and pleasant, but Arden still didn't feel comfortable with his having the run of the place. Did she dare risk offending him by asking for the key back? Or should she take the advice she'd given to Reid and have all the locks changed?

That wouldn't be a bad idea in any case, she decided. For all she knew, there could be any number of keys floating around. The notion that her grandfather might have gotten his hands on one was distinctly unnerving.

As she stood gazing into the greenhouse, her mind drifted back to her conversation with her uncle and how as a child he'd snuck out of his father's house every chance he got so that he could come here to Berdeaux Place. Arden could imagine him in the garden, peering through the glass walls of the greenhouse to watch his mother and sister as they happily worked among the plants. How lonely he must have been back then. How abandoned he must have felt. What could have happened in her grandparents' marriage to drive Evelyn away, taking her daughter and leaving her son behind to be raised by a cold, loveless man? How could any mother make that choice?

The answer was simple. She hadn't been given a choice.

And now Clement Mayfair wanted a relationship with Arden, his only granddaughter. After all these years, why the sudden interest in her welfare? The answer again was simple. She had something he wanted.

Maybe it was her imagination, but the breeze suddenly grew chilly as the shadows in the garden lengthened.

She turned away from the greenhouse, trusting that her mother's cereus wouldn't bloom for another few nights.

She paused again on her way back to the house, her gaze going once more to the summerhouse dome. Did she dare take a closer look? Once the sun went down, the light would fade quickly and she didn't want to be caught out in the garden at twilight. Orson Lee Finch was in prison and would likely remain there for the rest of his natural life, but another killer was out there somewhere. One who knew about the magnolia blossom that had been left on the summerhouse steps.

Arden approached those steps now with a curious blend of excitement and dread. She stood at the bottom, letting her gaze roam over the domed roof and the intricate latticework walls, peering up at the window from which her mother's killer had once stared back at her. Then she drew an unsteady breath as her mind went back to that twilight. She had stood then exactly where she stood now, her heart hammering against her chest. Her mother had lain motionless on the grass, her skin as pale as moonlight.

Even without the bloodstains on her mother's dress, Arden would have known that something truly horrible had happened. She hadn't fully understood that her mother was gone, not at first, but she knew she wanted nothing so much as to turn and run back to the safety of the house and into her grandmother's comforting embrace. A scent, a sound…a strange *knowing*…had held her in thrall until a scream finally bubbled up from her paralyzed throat. Then she hadn't been able to stop screaming even when help arrived, even when she'd been led back inside, away from the body, away from those disembodied eyes in the summerhouse window. She hadn't calmed down until her grandmother had sent for her best friend, Reid.

His father had brought him right over. Back then, he had always come when she needed him. *Some things don't change.*

The breeze was still warm, but Arden felt the deepest of chills. She hugged her arms to herself as she placed a foot on the bottom step. A rustling sound from inside the summerhouse froze her. Was someone in there?

More likely a squirrel or a bird, she told herself.

Still, she retreated back to the garden, rushing along the flagstone path, tripping as she glanced over her shoulder. No one was there, of course. That didn't stop her. She hurried inside and locked the door against the encroaching shadows. Then she unlocked the liquor cabinet and poured herself a shot of her grandmother's best whiskey.

Arden downed the fiery drink and poured another, carrying the glass with her upstairs to her bedroom. She turned on all the lights and searched through her closet until she found her secret stash—the reams of notes she and Reid had compiled during their summer investigation. They had only been children playing at detective, but even then they'd been resourceful and inquisitive. *Formidable.* It wasn't inconceivable that they may have stumbled across something important without realizing it.

Carrying everything back down to the front parlor,

she dropped to the floor and spread the notebooks around her on the rug. Imagining her grandmother's irritation at such a mess, she muttered a quick apology before digging in.

Thumbing through the pages, she marveled at how much time and attention a couple of twelve-year-olds had devoted to their endeavor. She finished her drink and poured another. She wasn't used to hard liquor and the whiskey soon went to her head. It was dark out by this time and she turned on a lamp before curling up on the sofa, leaving notebooks and markers strewn across the floor. It was too early to sleep. She would be up at the crack of dawn if she went to bed now. She would rest her eyes just for a few minutes. She would simply lie there very still as the room spun around her.

Sometime later, her eyes flew open, and for a moment she couldn't remember where she was. Then she wondered what had awakened her so abruptly. A sound…a smell…an instinct?

Just a dream, she told herself as she settled back against the couch. Nothing to worry about.

But she could hear something overhead…upstairs. Where exactly was the scrabbling sound coming from?

Bolting upright, she sat in the lamplight listening to the house. Berdeaux Place was over a hundred and fifty years old. Creaks and groans were to be expected. Nothing to worry about.

The sound came again, bringing her to her feet. Squirrels, she told herself. Just squirrels. *Nothing to worry about.*

A family of squirrels had once invaded the attic,

wreaking havoc on wiring and insulation until her grandmother had hired an exterminator. He'd trapped mother and babies and transported them to White Point Garden. At least that was the story Arden had been told.

She wasn't afraid of squirrels or mice, but she knew she wouldn't be able to sleep until she made sure nothing had found its way inside the house. Grabbing her grandmother's sword, she followed the sound out into the foyer. She wasn't sure what she hoped to accomplish with the blade. She certainly wouldn't run a poor squirrel through, but she liked to think she had enough grit to protect herself from an intruder. If nothing else, the feel of the curved hilt in her hand brought out her inner warrior woman. She went up the stairs without hesitation, pausing only at the top to listen.

Her grandmother's bedroom was at the front of the house, a large, airy room with an ancient, opulent en suite. Arden's room was at the back, with long windows that overlooked the garden. Her mother's room was across the hall.

Arden following the rummaging sound down the hallway, pausing only long enough to glance in her room. Everything was as she'd left it that morning. Bed neatly made up, suitcases unpacked, clothing all stored away.

She crossed to her mother's room, hovering in the hallway with her hand on the knob. After the murder, Arden's grandmother had locked the room, allowing only the housekeeper inside once a week to dust and vacuum. The room had become a mausoleum, abandoned and forbidden until Arden had gone to her grandmother and told her how much she hated the locked door. It was as if they were trying to lock their memories away, trying to forget her mother ever existed.

After that, the door had been opened, and Arden had been free to visit her mother's room whenever she desired. She used to spend hours inside, sitting by the windows or playing dress up in front of the long, gilded mirror. Sometimes she would just lie on the bed and stare at the ceiling as she drank in the lingering scent of her mother's candles.

Arden wasn't sure why she hesitated to go inside now. She wasn't afraid of ghosts. She wasn't afraid to remember her mother, whom she had loved with all her heart. She had a strange sense of guilt and displacement. Like she had been gone for so long she had no business violating this sacred place. Her emotions made little sense and felt irrational.

Taking a breath, she opened the door and stepped across the threshold. Moonlight flooded the room, glinting so brilliantly off the mirror that Arden was startled back into the hallway. Then she laughed at herself and reached for the light switch, her gaze roaming the room as she waited for her pulse to settle.

Her mother's domain was just as she'd left it all those years ago. The room was pretty and eclectic, bordering on Bohemian with the silk bed throw and thick floor pillows at all the windows. A suitable space for the mysterious young woman her mother had been. Arden could still smell the scented candles, but how was that possible? Surely the scent would have faded by now. Unless her grandmother had periodically replaced them. She may have even lit them from time to time.

Arden walked over to the dresser and lifted one of the candles to her nose. Sandalwood. The second was patchouli. The third...*magnolia*.

She was so shocked by the scent, she almost dropped the glass holder. Her fingers trembled, her heart pounded. She quickly set the candle aside. It's just a *scent*, she told herself. Nothing to worry about.

Hadn't she been the one who had talked her grandmother out of chopping down the magnificent old magnolia tree that shaded the summerhouse?

It's just a tree, Grandmother.

"It's just a scent," she whispered.

But the notion that someone other than her grandmother had been in her mother's room, burning a magnolia candle...

It *was* just a scent. Just a dream. Just squirrels...

Arden backtracked out of the room and closed the door. She hurried across the hall to her room, locking the door behind her and then shoving a chair up under the knob. She was safe enough at Berdeaux Place. The doors were all locked and the security system activated. No one could get in without her knowing.

She went over to the window to glance down into the garden. She could see the top of the summerhouse peeking through the trees and the glint of moonlight on the greenhouse. The night was still and calm, and yet she couldn't shake the scary notion that someone was down there hidden among the shadows. She'd once been expert at climbing down the trellis to escape her room. What if someone else had the notion to climb up? Was she really safe here?

She couldn't stand guard at the window all night. Neither could she close her eyes and fall back asleep. She was too keyed up now. Too wary of every night sound, no matter how slight.

Scouring the grounds one last time, she finally left the window and lay down on the bed, her grandmother's sword beside her. She thought again of Orson Lee Finch in prison, but the image of an aging killer behind bars gave her no comfort because another killer had already struck once. If someone wanted to set Reid up for murder, who better than her as his next victim?

She pulled the covers up over her and snuggled her head against the pillow, but she didn't fall asleep until dawn broke over the city and the light in her room turned golden.

Chapter Nine

Reid was already on his second cup of coffee by the time Arden arrived the next morning. The locksmith had come and gone and he was seated at his desk glancing through the paper as he chowed down on a breakfast burrito he'd bought at the corner store. He'd finally gotten a good night's sleep and felt better than he had in days. Arden, on the other hand, looked as if she hadn't slept a wink. The dark circles under her eyes had deepened and her response to his greeting had been lukewarm at best.

He gave her a lingering appraisal as she stood in his office doorway. "What's wrong?" he asked in concern. "You look like something the cat dragged in."

She gave him a pained smile. Then she glanced away as if she didn't want him to stare too deeply into her eyes. "I didn't get much sleep last night."

"I can tell." He took a quick sip of his coffee. "Anything I should know about?"

"Squirrels in the attic," she muttered.

Reid carefully set aside his cup. "Are you sure that's

all it was? Not residual nerves from what happened here yesterday?"

"I don't think so." Her gaze darted back to him and she shrugged. "Honestly, I think it's that house. I never imagined it would be so disconcerting to be there alone. Every time I go out into the garden, I remember what happened. I close my eyes and I picture my mother's body, so cold and still, on the ground. I imagine someone staring back at me from the summerhouse windows."

"You lived in that house for years after your mother died," Reid said. "You never seemed to dwell on it back then."

She brushed back her hair with a careless gesture. "I was a kid. I thought I was invincible. Plus, I had you."

His heart gave a funny little jump. "No one is invincible."

"I've never been more aware of that fact since you came to my house the other evening and told me about the latest murder. And speaking of invincible..." She glanced over her shoulder toward the entrance. "I noticed you had the locks changed. That was fast."

"I have a friend in the business. He sent someone out first thing this morning. I don't want a repeat of what happened yesterday."

"That's smart," she said with a nod. "I've been thinking it would be a good idea to change the locks at Berdeaux Place, as well. If my uncle has a key to the side gate, then he may also have one to the house. And if he has a key to the house—"

"Your grandfather could gain access," Reid finished.

"I'll set you up with my friend. You can trust him. I've known him for years. In fact, he was one of my first clients. You should also have him check out your security system, make sure everything is up-to-date. At the very least, you need to change your code."

"I've already done that." She had remained hovering in the doorway of his office all this time; now she came in and dumped the contents of her tote bag on his desk.

He took in the black-and-white notebooks and then glanced up. "What's all this?"

"Don't you recognize them?" Arden sat down in a chair across from his desk. She wore white jeans and a summery top that left her toned arms bare. Her hair was down today and tucked behind her ears. He caught the glitter of tiny diamonds in her lobes, could smell the barest hint of honeysuckle as she settled into her chair. "They're the notebooks from our investigation," she explained.

He picked one out of the pile and opened the cover. "I can't believe you kept these things."

"Why wouldn't I? We worked really hard that summer. I know it's mostly kid stuff, but we actually uncovered some interesting details. For instance, do you remember that Orson Lee Finch once worked down the street from Berdeaux Place?"

"As I recall, he worked for a number of families that resided in the Historic District. He was a well-regarded gardener at one time."

"Yes, but I somehow let all that slip my mind. Deliberately so, perhaps. Grandmother even hired him a few times to do some of the heavy chores that her aging gardener couldn't manage. I vaguely remember Finch. He was a short, thin man with kind eyes and a sweet smile. He once gave me a stick of gum."

"Ted Bundy was a real charmer, too," Reid said as he rifled through a few pages of the notebook. "What's your point?"

"I'm just pointing out that he had ample opportunity to acquaint himself with my mother's circumstances and habits. He had ample opportunity to watch me, too. But then so did a lot of other people. And who's to say the real killer didn't have occasion to observe Finch's circumstances and habits and determine he'd make a good patsy?"

"'The real killer'? 'A patsy'?" Reid gave her a skeptical look.

"If we're working from our old theory that Finch was framed." She reached over and plucked one of the notebooks from Reid's desk. "I went through some of the pages last night and highlighted the entries that caught my eye. When you have time, you might want to take a closer look, too."

"Why?" Reid closed the notebook and set it aside. He had also been doing a lot of thinking since last night. She wasn't going to like what he had to say.

"Why?" She stared him down. "Because a young woman was murdered down the block from where we sit. You said yourself the location of your office and the magnolia blossom left at the crime scene link us to the murder."

"Link *us*. But that doesn't mean there's a connection to your mother's murder. That's a long shot in my opinion."

Arden's expression turned suspicious. "What's going on with you? Why do you keep saying one thing and then five minutes later say the opposite? My head is spinning trying to keep up with you."

He'd be frustrated, too, if he were in her position, but she'd thrown him off his game. He'd said things he shouldn't have and made rash decisions that weren't in either of their best interests. Time to rectify his mistakes. "Unlike you, I got plenty of rest last night. My head is clearer than it's been in days. I'm trying to look at the situation rationally instead of emotionally."

"Okay. But what would be the harm in at least glancing through our notes?" Arden asked. "Who knows? We might find something that would help us with your current predicament."

"By current predicament, I assume you mean Dave Brody. I don't see how."

"If Finch really was framed, maybe the same person is now trying to frame you."

"Arden."

"Don't Arden me. We'll never get to the bottom of anything unless you keep an open mind. But forget about the notebooks for a moment." She sat forward, eyes gleaming. "I think I've figured how we can find Ginger Vreeland."

Reid wrapped up his half-eaten burrito carefully and set it aside.

"Don't you at least want to hear my idea?"

"I don't think so." He folded his arms on the desk

and tried to remain resolved. "I've done some thinking, too, and I've decided it's a bad idea to involve you in my problems. We have to be smart about this. If someone is trying to set me up, they wouldn't hesitate to come after you if they thought you were in the way."

"I can take care of myself," she insisted. "Besides that, has it not occurred to you that the killer may come after me whether I'm helping you or not? What better way to frame you for murder than to take out an old girlfriend? Think about that, Reid. There's safety in numbers. We need to stick together. And you need someone you can trust watching your back."

She had a point, but that someone didn't need to be her. *If anything happened to Arden—*

He banished the thought before it could take root.

"I appreciate your enthusiasm. I do. But you need to keep your distance. At least for now."

She rolled her eyes in frustration. "There you go again. Changing your mind on a dime. I don't get you, Reid Sutton. We had all of this resolved yesterday afternoon. What's changed?"

"I'm trying to do what's best for both of us." *Don't back down. And don't get distracted by her I'm-so-disappointed-in-you look.* The disapproval in her eyes meant nothing to him. This was his house, his business. He had a right to make whatever decisions he deemed necessary. "Why do you want to work here anyway? Don't you have better things to do with your time?"

"Such as?"

"You said you wanted to oversee the renovations to Berdeaux Place because you don't trust anyone else.

You even mentioned your plan to take on some of the work yourself. Do you have any idea how time-consuming a project like that can be?"

"Of course I do. I also know I'll go out of my mind if I have to stay in that house twenty-four hours a day."

He picked up a pen and examined the barrel. "Then why not get a job in your field? There are any number of museums and art galleries in this city that would jump at the chance to have someone with your expertise."

"Not a one of them will touch me," she said.

He glanced up. "What?"

She met his gaze boldly. "You heard me. The places you mentioned won't hire me."

"Why not?"

She hesitated, her defiance wilting under cross-examination. "I wasn't altogether truthful with you the other night about the reason I left my job."

"You were fired?"

She sighed. "Try not to gloat? This is hard enough without that smirk."

He didn't think he was gloating or smirking, but he apologized anyway. "Sorry. Go on."

"I wasn't fired. I resigned before it came to that. But just barely," she admitted.

"What happened?"

She entwined her fingers in her lap. "The museum was sold several months ago. The new owners brought in some of their own staff, including a new director. He was funny, handsome, charismatic. We found we had a lot in common. We liked the same music, read the same books. We became friends. Close friends."

"Is that what they're calling it these days?" Reid had a sudden, inexplicable pain in his chest. He sat up straighter, as if good posture could make the ache go away.

"Call it whatever you like. A friendship. A relationship." She dropped her gaze. "An intense flirtation."

The knife twisted as Reid remained silent.

She fixated on her tangled fingers. "Turns out he was married."

Stab me again, why don't you? "You had an affair with a married man?" He hadn't meant to sound so aghast or judgmental. He hardly had the moral ground here, but still. This was Arden.

She looked up at his tone. "It wasn't an affair. It was never physical. Not *that* physical and I had no idea he was married. Maybe I didn't want to know. But looking back, there were no obvious clues or signs. Nothing that would give him away. He was that good. Or maybe I was just that stupid." Color tinged her cheeks. "Anyway, I later learned that he and his wife had been separated for a time. She followed him to Atlanta and they reconciled. When she got wind of our…"

"Intense flirtation."

Arden's blush deepened. "She stormed into the museum one day and made a scene. She was very upset. Overwrought. You can't even imagine the things she said to me."

"Oh, I bet I can."

"She was under the impression that I was the one who had come on to her husband. When he rejected my advances, I became aggressive. He told her I *stalked* him."

"Wow."

Arden nodded. "Her accusations blindsided me. I don't consider myself naive, but I was completely fooled."

"Sounds like a real catch, this guy."

She frowned. "It's not funny, Reid."

No, but if he didn't make light of the situation, he might get on the first flight to Atlanta, track this guy down and do something really stupid. "No one who knows you would ever believe such a ridiculous claim."

She gave a weak shrug. "My friends stuck by me, but I was humiliated in front of my coworkers and damaged in the eyes of the new owners. I had no choice but to leave."

"So you came back home to lick your wounds," Reid said.

"Something like that. You see now why I can't apply for a job in my field? The moment anyone calls for a reference, all that ugliness follows me here."

Reid flexed his fingers and tried to relax. "Why didn't you tell me any of this yesterday?"

"It's a hard thing to talk about. It goes against the image I've always had of myself. Strong. Independent. Fearless. The truth of the matter is, I'm none of those things." She glanced out the window before she turned back to Reid. "Do you want to hear something else about me? Another dark truth about Arden Mayfair?"

"Always."

"I'd been spinning my wheels in the same position

forever. I only ever became friends with him because I thought he could help advance my career. Turns out, I'm not such a great catch, either."

"I don't know about that," Reid said. "I can name about a dozen guys right here in Charleston who would disagree with you."

Her gaze burned into his, begging the question: *Are you one of them?*

Reid refused to speak on the grounds he might incriminate himself.

She gave him a tentative smile. The same smile that had held him enthralled since they were four years old. The same smile that had once made him believe he could climb mountains and slay dragons on her behalf.

She broke the silence with another question. "How is it that you always know the right thing to say?" she asked softly.

"It seems to me I've been saying the wrong thing ever since you came back. The one thing I do know is that everyone makes mistakes. Even you. You pick yourself up and you move on. That's all you can do."

"Is that what you did after we split up?"

"Yes, after a while. But we're talking about you right now."

She nodded. "It wasn't my intent to come here yesterday and ask you for a job. I wanted your legal advice. That's all. Then I saw this house…" She glanced around the messy office, lifting her gaze to the stained ceiling before returning her focus to Reid. "I understand your vision for this place. I got it the minute I walked through the door. An unpretentious but respectable neighborhood law firm where ordinary, everyday people in need can come in without fear of rejection or intimidation. In other words, the antithesis of Sutton & Associates."

"And here I thought my vision was just to keep this place afloat."

"You can play it off that way, but I know you have big plans for this firm. Whether you want to admit it or not, I can help you. I'm smart—at least most of the time—and you won't find a harder worker. But you have to get over the antiquated notion that I need to be protected. I'm a big girl, Reid."

"Oh, I know."

"Then what's it to be? Should I leave now, never again to darken your door? Or should I sit right here and tell you how we can smoke Ginger Vreeland out of her hiding place?"

He had already lost the battle and they both knew it. The trick now was to salvage as much of the war as he could. "If we're going to do this, we need to set some ground rules."

"Okay."

He looked her right in the eyes. "This is my house, my firm. I have the final say. If I don't want to take on a particular client, we don't take on that client. If I say something is too dangerous to pursue, that's the end of it."

"Of course."

His gaze narrowed. "That was too easy."

"Maybe," she agreed with a conciliatory smile. "I want this to work, but we have to be realistic. We're both stubborn, impulsive, passionate people. We're bound to clash now and then. But I do agree that when it comes to this firm, you have the final say."

"Then why do I feel like I've just been snookered," he muttered.

"This will work out for both of us. You'll see." She scooted to the edge of her seat. "*Now* do you want to hear about my plan?"

"I'm pretty sure I don't have a choice."

She gave him a brilliant smile, one without arrogance or guile. "It may sound a little convoluted at first, so just hear me out. I studied the file you gave me yesterday, in particular the transcript of Ginger Vreeland's interview. She was once married. Did you know that? She married right out of high school and her husband joined the service a month later. They divorced when he came back from overseas. He died some years back in a motorcycle accident. Her closest living relative is an uncle who lives just outside of town. He practically raised her when her mother would be off on a bender. If anyone knows where she is now, it would be this uncle."

Reid stared at her for a moment. "You got all that from the file I gave you?"

"Yes, didn't you read through it?"

"Not as closely as you did, apparently, but let me see if I can contribute to the conversation. Brody said he'd hired a private detective while he was in prison, someone he'd known in the joint. According to this guy, Ginger's family still wouldn't talk. I'm assuming that includes the uncle."

Arden wasn't the least bit thwarted. If anything, she

became more animated. "Then we have to give him an incentive. I thought of something last night when I couldn't sleep."

"Of course you did." Reid couldn't believe this was the same aloof woman he'd confronted on Sunday night. His accusation that she'd become pedestrian over the years suddenly rang hollow. She hadn't changed. Maybe, deep down, he hadn't either. He wasn't sure if that was a good thing or not. But her excitement was infectious and he found himself leaning forward, anticipating her every word.

"A few years ago, I was part of a class action suit against a bank that had opened unauthorized accounts in some of their customers' names. Something like that has been in the news recently with a much larger bank on a much larger scale, but the premise was the same. I was barely even aware of the suit until I was notified that money from the settlement had been deposited into my account. It was only a few hundred dollars, but that's beside the point." She paused to tuck back her hair. "What if we contact Ginger's uncle and tell him that Ginger is still listed as her dead ex-husband's beneficiary? His bank account is considered inactive and unless she acts quickly, she won't be able to claim the money from the settlement. The amount would have to be large enough to tempt her out of hiding, yet not so large as to arouse her suspicions. We'll say our firm specializes in helping people collect forgotten money. For a finder's fee, we'll file all the necessary paperwork to have the funds released to her, but we need to speak with her in person to verify her identity."

"In other words, we lie," Reid said.

"Yes, but would you rather Dave Brody find her first?" Arden asked. "We may be lying but we know we won't hurt her. We can't say the same about him. We'll leave the uncle a business card and tell him time is of the essence."

Reid ran fingers through his hair. "You're right about one thing. This scheme is plenty convoluted."

"It can work, though."

"Maybe, but I see at least one glaring problem. She's bound to recognize my name."

"Then I'll be the contact person. I'll have some business cards printed up with a burner phone number. The name Mayfair might even carry a little weight. I can put up a website, too. Simple but classy. Should only take a couple of days to get everything set up."

"If Ginger suspects a con, it could drive her even deeper underground," he said.

"That's just a chance we'll have to take. And it's still preferable to Brody finding her first."

Reid was silent for a moment as he ran the scenario through his head. "You say you can get this all set up in just two days' time?"

"Yes, if I put in some overtime, but I'll need a place to work." She glanced in the other room. "I can't sit on the floor all day."

"I'll get you a desk," Reid said. "In the meantime, you can use mine. I'll be out for most of the day anyway. That is, if you're sure you'll be okay here alone."

"I feel safer here than I do at Berdeaux Place. You've

had the locks changed and I won't let anyone in while you're gone. I'll be fine."

"You'll need this." He handed her a key.

She looked surprised. "I thought you said you didn't give out keys to anyone."

"Just take it, Arden."

Chapter Ten

Reid had been gone for a few hours when Arden decided to take a lunch break. Since the fridge was pretty much empty, she walked down to a little café on Queen Street that offered a delicious array of wraps and salads. She made her selection and then perused her notes as she ate. She didn't dawdle once she finished and, instead, stuffed everything back into her bag and quickly paid the check. She was just stepping outside when someone across the street caught her attention. Arden recognized him immediately as the man Reid had spoken to the day before. Dave Brody.

Her heart skipped a beat and she started to retreat back into the eatery while she waited for him to pass. But he seemed oblivious to her presence. He had his phone to his ear and appeared agitated by the conversation. He gestured with his free arm and then rubbed a hand across his buzzed head in apparent frustration. Even after he returned the phone to his pocket, he continued to rail at the air and then gestured menacingly at a passerby before he stomped off down the street.

Arden decided he must be heading to Reid's office,

and she told herself just to wait inside the café until he'd put plenty of distance between them. Why take a chance on being seen? Hadn't she promised Reid she would be careful?

Still, an opportunity had presented itself. Brody had spent hours watching Reid's place and tailing him around town. Why not turn the tables? She could follow at a discreet distance and observe his behavior and interactions. If he tried to break into the house, she would call the police.

Fishing her sunglasses out of her bag, she slipped them on as she waited underneath the awning to make sure he didn't turn around. But she didn't want him to get too far ahead, so she fell in behind a family of five strolling by. The two adults and tallest child would provide enough cover so that if Brody happened to glance back, he wouldn't be able to see her. That worked for about two blocks and then the family turned a corner, leaving Arden exposed. She hugged the inside edge of the sidewalk, hoping the shade of the buildings would somewhat protect her.

What are you doing, Arden? What on earth are you thinking?

She shoved the voice aside as she hooked her bag over her shoulder and kept walking. Somewhere in the back of her mind, a plan took shape. What if Brody really was working for someone powerful who wanted to frame Reid for murder? What if he was on his way to meet that person right now? It was a long shot and not without risk, but wouldn't it be something if she could solve this whole mystery simply by tailing Brody to his final destination? The trick was to stay out of his periphery. It was broad daylight and traffic was fairly brisk. *Just don't let him get so far ahead of you that he can double back without your knowing.*

They were headed west on Queen Street. If his final destination had been Reid's office, he would have turned right on Logan, but instead he kept going all the way to Rutledge, finally turning left on Wentworth. Then came a series of quick turns onto side streets that left Arden completely disoriented. She didn't know the area well and might have thought Brody was deliberately trying to lose her, but from everything Reid had told her, evasion was hardly Brody's style. He was more likely to turn around and confront her openly.

Still, she widened the distance between them, trying to blend into the scenery as best she could. He made another turn and she finally recognized where they were. The houses along the street had seen better days, but the yards were shady, and every now and then, the breeze carried the scent of jasmine over garden fences.

Traffic dwindled and Arden crossed the street to trail behind a pair of college students, who undoubtedly lived in one of the nearby apartment complexes. Up ahead, Brody stopped in front of a two-story house with a wrought-iron fence encasing the front walkway and garden. Arden broke away from the students and darted into an alley, where she could watch Brody from a safe distance. As he opened the gate and stepped into the garden, a middle-aged woman wearing shorts and a baggy T-shirt came down the porch steps to confront him.

Their raised voices carried across to the alley, but Arden could make out only a word now and then of the argument, something about late rent. The woman, presumably Brody's landlady, gestured toward the outside staircase that led up to a second-story apartment. Brody became so agitated that Arden worried he might actually assault the poor woman.

Although she braced herself to intervene, the disagreement never became physical. Brody headed up the stairs and disappeared inside the door at the top of the landing. He came back out a few minutes later and flung money at the woman. She screamed an oath and then scrambled to grab the bills before the breeze carried them away. Brody watched her for a moment, then turned on his heel and exited the gate, heading back up the street the way he'd come.

Arden pressed herself against the wall, trying to disappear into the shadows until he was safely past the alley. Then she glanced up the street. She could still see him in the distance. She would have left the alley to follow except for the woman across the street, who had once again caught her attention. She plucked the last of the bills from the ground, folded the wad and tucked it into her shorts pocket. Then she came through the gate and stood on the sidewalk, hand shading her eyes as she watched Brody's receding form. Once he rounded a corner, she went back inside the fence and marched up the stairs, pausing on the landing to glance over her shoulder. Satisfied that she was alone, she retrieved a key from a flowerpot and let herself into the apartment.

By this time, Brody was long gone. As much as

Arden wanted to try to catch up with him, she was intrigued by the woman's behavior. She waited in the shadows, her gaze fixated on the door at the top of the stairs. The woman reappeared a few minutes later, glanced around once more to make sure no one had seen her and returned the key to the flowerpot. She came down the stairs and rounded the house to the porch. A moment later Arden heard a door slam.

Leaning back against the building, she placed a hand over her pounding heart. The adrenaline pulsating through her veins was a rush she hadn't experienced in years. She was reminded of the time she and Reid had taken his father's boat out for a midnight sail. They'd stayed on the water all night, drunk with freedom and adventure as they contemplated how far they dared go before turning back.

Now, a little voice goaded her. *Now is the time to turn back.*

Arden once again ignored that voice.

Leaving the alley, she glanced both ways before crossing the street. Without hesitation, she made for the garden gate, rehearsing in her mind what she would say if she were caught. She wasn't so worried about the landlady. Arden had always been able to think on her feet. She'd make up an excuse about having the wrong address or looking for an old friend. Brody was a different story. She'd glimpsed his temper and had no doubt he was dangerous. Now, though, she was more convinced than ever that he had to be working for someone. The area was seedy, but apartments this close to downtown didn't come cheap no matter the neighborhood.

How could she pass up this chance? Someone was trying to set Reid up for murder. What if she could determine the identity of the real killer by searching Brody's possessions? What if she could prove Reid's innocence once and for all? Wasn't he worth taking that risk?

On and on, the devil on her shoulder goaded her.

Arden knew what Reid would say. He'd tell her to go back to the office and lock the doors. Hunker down until he returned later that afternoon. But cowering inside locked doors wouldn't help him out of his current predicament. There'd been a time when he would have applauded her efforts.

In a way, she was doing this as much for herself as for him, Arden decided. She wanted to be that girl again. The one who threw caution to the wind and followed her heart.

Let's not get carried away.

She found the key in the flowerpot, unlocked the door and then returned the key, using her foot to hold open the door. She slipped inside and took off her sunglasses. The apartment was dim and overly warm. Or maybe she was just overly excited. A scene from one of her favorite movies came to mind. A determined young woman risking life and limb to get the goods on a murderer so she could prove to her adventurous lover she was more than his match.

Focus, Arden. You are not Grace Kelly. And this is not a movie.

She stood with her back against the closed door and drew in air as she tried to quiet her thundering heart. Then her gaze darted about the small space, taking it all in before she began to explore. To the left of the entrance was a tiny bathroom; to the right, a bedroom. The narrow foyer opened directly into a living area and the kitchen was just through an archway. The space was tight but efficient.

Her gaze lit on a wooden table beneath the only window in the living room. An expensive laptop and printer were set up, along with a flat-screen TV. How did someone fresh out of prison afford such expensive devices?

She moved across the room as silently as she could manage on aging floorboards. After taking a quick peek through a stack of papers on the table, she turned her attention to the laptop. It opened to the desktop and she navigated to the Pictures folder, scanning dozens of thumbnails before she found the incriminating photos of Reid. Brody must have been following him for days. He'd captured Reid through his office window, at the courthouse on Broad Street, on the sidewalk in front of Berdeaux Place. When she reached the images from the bar, Arden grew even more agitated. The angle of some of the shots made it look as though Reid and the victim were interacting.

Arden could have spent hours examining every nuance of those photographs, but she'd already spent too much time in Brody's apartment. She'd pressed her luck long enough. Panic had set in so she did the only thing she could think of in the moment. She attached the images to an email and sent them to her account. Then she deleted the message from the Sent folder. *What else? What else?* Grabbing a tissue from her bag, she wiped down the computer and anything else in the vicinity she might have touched.

She was just finishing up when she heard footsteps on the wooden stairs outside the apartment. Quickly she gathered up her bag and took one last look at the table, then hurried to peek out the front widow.

Brody was coming up the stairs. He was almost at the landing.

Arden cast a frantic glance around and then darted inside the tiny bathroom. She flattened herself in the tub and pulled the shower curtain closed.

The door opened and Brody came inside the apartment. She listened as he clomped through the rooms, praying he wouldn't need to use the bathroom or, even worse, decide to take a shower.

A ringtone sounded and he answered with an impatient grunt.

"Yeah, yeah, I know I'm late. Unforeseen circumstances."

Arden heard a drawer slide open. She hadn't left anything on the table, had she? She hadn't moved his laptop enough so that he would notice? She squeezed her eyes closed and waited. Into the silence came the metallic click of what she imagined to be a switchblade. She pictured him testing the vicious blade with his thumb as he glanced toward the bathroom...

"Relax, dude. I'm on my way now. You just make sure you have the money."

He left the apartment and slammed the door behind him. Arden waited to make sure he wasn't coming back, and then she climbed shuddering out of the tub. She went back over to the table to make sure nothing was amiss and quickly exited the apartment.

By the time she got to the street, Brody was well ahead of her. She accelerated her pace, trying to shorten the distance between them without calling attention to herself. He strode along, a man on a mission, turning here, turning there until they finally reached King Street and she lost him.

Arden came to a stop, glancing up and down the street. The sidewalks were crowded for a weekday, but his appearance would make him stand out among the tourists and shoppers. Maybe he'd gone inside one of the boutiques. That hardly seemed likely, but he couldn't have just vanished.

As she stood there contemplating where he might have gone, a hand fell on her shoulder.

She jumped and turned with a gasp. Her arm went back in self-defense. Instead of swinging her bag at Brody's head, she said incredulously, "Uncle Calvin! What are you doing here?"

A smile flashed, disarming her instantly. "I was just about to ask you the same thing, but then I assumed you'd come for a tour of the studio."

She tried to act natural as she dropped the bag to her side and smoothed back her hair. "Actually, I was just out doing a little shopping. Although if I'd known the address of your studio, I would have stopped by."

He motioned to a building across the street. "I'm

on the second floor. Lots of beautiful light. Come up. I'll fix you something cold to drink and give you the grand tour."

"That sounds lovely." Arden shot a glance over her shoulder before she followed her uncle across the street and up to his studio. Despite the heat, he looked cool and collected in khaki chinos and a cotton shirt that complemented his eyes and the white-gold hair that curled at his collar.

Arden marveled at how young he looked for his age. A stranger would never have guessed that he was well into his forties. It was only when he turned at the top of the stairs and gave her a little smile that she noticed the crinkles at the corners of his eyes and the deeper crevices in his brow. "It's a working studio," he said. "Nothing too fancy and it's a bit of a mess right now. I've been inspired lately and painting like a madman."

"I'm eager to see it."

He stepped back for her to enter, and she stood gazing around. The space was wide open, with an industrial flavor from the original plank flooring, brick walls and long windows that reached to the beamed ceiling. Canvases were stacked at least three deep along the walls and an easel had been set up to take advantage of the morning sunlight.

"It's a wonderful space," Arden said as she moved into the center of the room. "Bigger than I imagined, and the light really is beautiful. So soft and golden. I can see how you'd be inspired here."

"It's not the studio that inspires me, though I do consider myself lucky for having found this place," Calvin said. "It's one of a kind."

"How long have you been here?"

"A while."

"You mentioned that you live nearby?"

"Only a few blocks away. It's very convenient."

Arden walked over to one of the windows that looked down on the street. "If I had this studio, I don't think I'd ever want to leave."

"You haven't seen my apartment," he said with another smile.

"That's true."

"Minuscule compared to Mayfair House, but it suits my needs perfectly."

"I've decided big homes are overrated," Arden said. "Not to mention overwhelming."

"Yes. We tend to take those grand old places and all the accompanying creature comforts for granted when someone else is footing the bill. But there is something to be said for freedom." His gaze darkened before he reclaimed his good humor. "Anyway, you'll have to come to dinner soon. I'm not a bad cook."

"That would be nice. Just let me get settled first."

"Of course. In the meantime, what will you have to drink? I have iced tea, lemonade…"

"Iced tea is perfect."

He disappeared into another room. "Make yourself at home," he called out. "I'll be right back."

"Is it okay if I look at your paintings?"

"Certainly. Nothing in the studio is off-limits."

She wandered around the perimeter of the room,

examining the canvases and admiring the iconic land-marks that he had painted. The church towers, the cemeteries, the pastel homes on Rainbow Row. Even Berdeaux Place. The paintings were colorful, the subject matter dear to Arden's heart, and yet an inexplicable melancholy descended. She was home now. She could visit any of these places whenever she liked. But study-ing her uncle's art was like observing her beloved city through a mist. There was an unsettling disconnec-tion. Was that how Calvin had felt as a child visiting Berdeaux Place? A lonely little boy observing from a distance a happier life that should have been his?

She shrugged, dismissing the thought, deciding it was best to leave the psychoanalysis to the experts.

Circling the room, she finally came to a stop in front of the easel. The unfinished painting jolted her. She blinked and then blinked again. It was like her previ-ous thoughts had suddenly materialized.

"You've painted Mother's cereus." *Through a green-house window. From the outside peering in.*

"I've attempted to. It's a rather complicated plant. The texture of the leaves is tricky."

"Are you kidding me? The detail is amazing," Arden said in wonder.

"Thank you for that." He came back into the room and handed her a frosty glass. "I'll paint a companion piece once the blooms have opened. That is, if you have no objection."

"Of course not. Your work is very beautiful and you seem to be quite prolific. I had no idea." She glanced around the room at all the canvases. "Do you paint everything from memory?"

"Not always. I sketch and sometimes I work from photographs."

"This painting almost looks like a photograph. I feel as if I'm gazing through the greenhouse window." She took a sip of tea as she gave him a sidelong glance. "I went out to the garden last night, but I didn't see you working."

"I didn't want to disturb you again. Besides, there's little point in coming every night until the blooms are further along."

"I can't get over the colors," Arden murmured, her attention still on the cereus. "It's almost as if…" She trailed away, shy about her thoughts all of a sudden.

"As if…what?"

"You'll think I'm crazy."

Her uncle smiled. "Artists are by nature crazy. Who am I to judge?"

Still, Arden hesitated. "It's like Grandmother is there in the greenhouse. Mother, too. You didn't paint them. You can't see them. But I can feel them."

He drew a sharp breath.

"I'm sorry," Arden said. "Did I say something wrong?"

"No, quite the opposite, in fact. It's just so rare to find someone who feels about your work the way you do. You couldn't have known what was in my heart or in my head when I painted that scene and yet…" Now he was the one who broke off. "Forgive me. I'm just… I'm blown away by your insight." He walked over to the easel and picked up the canvas. "I think you must have this."

"Oh, I couldn't. As beautiful as it is, I can't take your work."

"Why not? I'm offering it to you as a gift. Although…" He returned the canvas to the easel. "I have one that you might appreciate more." He set his drink aside and disappeared through another doorway. He returned carrying a small canvas, which he offered to Arden. "My welcome-home gift to you. I hope you like this one as much as I do. And before you say anything, I won't take no for an answer."

Arden went very still as he turned the painting and she got her first glimpse of the subject. Uneasiness crept over her as she took the canvas from his hands and turned toward the light. He had painted her mother in the moonlit garden at Berdeaux Place with the summerhouse dome in the background. Camille Mayfair looked just as Arden remembered her. The mysterious glint in her eyes. The dazzling smile. But there was a feeling of distance again. The perception of admiring her from afar.

The red chiffon gown she wore appeared so soft and airy that Arden could almost imagine the frothy layers floating up from the canvas. Camille's bare arms and shoulders gleamed softly in the moonlight and her blond hair was pulled back and fastened with a creamy magnolia blossom.

A magnolia blossom.

Arden was speechless.

"Do you like it?" her uncle asked softly. "I tried to catch her whimsy and drama, but I'm not that talented."

"No, you are. It's wonderful. I can't stop looking at her." Arden tried to swallow past the sudden knot in her throat.

Calvin seemed overcome, as well. "Now you know why I was so taken aback when I saw you standing in the moonlight the other night."

Arden couldn't tear her gaze from the canvas. "When did you paint this?"

"A few years ago from a photograph that was taken on the night of the Mayor's Ball. It was held at Berdeaux Place that year. I was away at school, but I remember reading about it in the paper."

"I remember it, too," Arden said. "She came into my room before she went downstairs. She looked like a princess in that red dress. I can still remember the way the magnolia blossom smelled in her hair when she leaned over the bed to kiss me good-night. A few days later, she was gone."

Calvin gently took the canvas from her fingers. "I'll wrap this up and have it delivered to the house."

Arden glanced up. "Are you sure?"

"I couldn't bear for anyone but you to have it," he said.

"I don't know what to say. Thank you, Uncle."

"You're welcome, Niece. I have something else for you, too." He placed the canvas on his worktable and took a key from a peg on the wall. "This is the key to the side gate. It was one thing for me to come and go as I pleased when no one was in the house, but the last thing I want to do is intrude on your privacy."

He offered her the key and she took it without argument. "That's very thoughtful of you. Actually, I've been thinking about having all the locks changed. The house has been empty for so long. Who knows how many keys may be floating around?"

Something flashed in his eyes, an emotion that unnerved Arden even more than the painting had. "Probably a good idea," he murmured. "Your safety is paramount."

His mood had changed, though. Arden couldn't figure out what had happened. Maybe he had expected her to refuse the key or to at least offer a token resistance. In any case, it was time for her to leave.

"I should be going. I've taken up enough of your time. Thank you for showing me your studio. As for the painting…" She trailed away. "You have no idea what it means to me."

"I'm glad that it makes you happy." He walked her to the top of the stairs.

"I can see myself down," she said. "Thank you again."

"Come back soon. I've a lot more to show you."

"I'll do that." She went down the stairs without looking back, but when she crossed the street, she couldn't help glancing up at the studio. He stood at one of the long windows staring down at her.

Chapter Eleven

Reid approached the house on Water Street on foot. He'd parked a block over so that his car wouldn't be spotted entering or leaving the driveway. He opened the wrought-iron gate and strode up the walkway to the front door, glancing over his shoulder as he rang the bell. His mother played bridge on Wednesdays and the housekeeper had the day off. He expected the house to be empty, but he still had a key and the security code unless either or both had been changed since his last visit.

He waited a few minutes and then let himself in, disarming the system as he called out to his mother. Then he called out the housekeeper's name. "Anyone home?" He folded his sunglasses and slipped them in his pocket as his gaze traveled up the curving staircase. Nothing stirred. The house was empty except for the ghosts.

Still, he felt uneasy being in his childhood home uninvited. He tried to shake off his disquiet as he headed to the back of the house where his father's office was located, a rich, masculine room that looked out on the pool. The drapes were open and Reid could see the dance of sunlight on blue water as he stepped through the pocket doors. He had no idea what he was looking for. His father's equivalent of a little black book, he supposed. The heavy oak desk was kept locked, but Reid had known since he was a kid that the key rested on a ledge underneath the smooth top.

Plopping down in his father's chair, he felt underneath the desk until he located the key. He was just about to open the top drawer when he heard a car pull up outside. He returned the key to the ledge and got up from the desk, slipping silently into the hallway. He heard the back door close and then someone moving about in the kitchen. Maybe Tess had changed her day off, Reid thought, and he quickly came up with an excuse for his presence as he eased down the corridor.

The kitchen was spacious with gleaming stainless steel appliances and a marble island large enough to accommodate six people. His father stood behind the counter splashing whiskey into a tumbler. Watching him from the doorway, Reid wondered if he was catching a glimpse of his future. The notion was hardly comforting. His father had never been an easy man to know or love. He was brilliant and wildly successful, but he'd never struck Reid as particularly happy, which had not made for a particularly happy household. Yet, despite Boone's failings as a parent and husband, he'd always taken as his due the devotion and respect of those around him.

But credit where credit was due, the man seemed committed to keeping the years at bay. He was as sharp and ruthless as ever, and he kept himself in excellent physical shape. Reid would give him that. He worked out, played tennis twice a week and watched his diet. A cocktail in the middle of the day seemed out of character, but how well did Reid really know his father?

He cleared his throat and Boone looked up in surprise.

"What the hell are you doing here?" he demanded.

"I came to see Mother."

"Your mother has had a standing bridge date every Wednesday for the past thirty years. You know that as well as I do."

"I guess it slipped my mind," Reid said.

His father frowned at him over the rim of his glass. "How did you get in here anyway?"

Reid sauntered into the kitchen. "I still have a key. You disowned me. Mother didn't."

Boone scoffed as he downed his drink. "Disowned is a little dramatic."

"Is it? Let's recap. You had Security escort me from the building after you fired me, and then you stood on the sidewalk and told me that I was no son of yours, that I would never see a penny of inheritance and that I shouldn't even think about trying to capitalize on the Sutton name. I'd say that's pretty much the dictionary definition of *disowned*, but we can agree to disagree." Reid hadn't realized until that moment how much his father's words still rankled. He'd convinced himself the estrangement was for the best. Time away from the old man suited him just fine. But no son, no matter his age, wanted to be ostracized by his father. A tiny part of Reid still craved a word of encouragement, no matter how fleeting.

"I was angry," Boone said. "And you were insubordinate and disrespectful. I treated you as I would have any other associate."

"I was trying to protect my client. The client you ordered me to drop because one of your cronies had a problem with my representing a man he considered an upstart competitor. Whatever happened to loyalty?"

"Some might say I'm loyal to a fault," his father countered. "That crony, as you call him, has thrown more work my way than you'll ever see in a lifetime. So I made a judgment call. My firm, my decision."

Had he sounded like that much of a pompous ass with Arden that morning? Reid wondered. The term *like father, like son* had never grated more.

His father glanced up from his drink. "You know what your problem is?"

"No, but I'm sure you're dying to tell me."

"You're too much like your mother. You personalize everything and then you cling to your grudges. Me? I let off steam and then I move on."

"You've moved on?"

"Water under the bridge." His father got down a second glass. "Come have a drink with me."

"It's a little early for me," Reid said as he straddled one of the bar stools.

"What's the saying…? It has to be five o'clock somewhere." Boone poured a whiskey and slid the glass across the island.

Reid cradled the tumbler in both hands, but he

didn't drink. "What are you doing home at this time of day anyway?"

Boone shrugged. "I needed a quiet place to work. You know how it gets around the office. So much going on you can't hear yourself think."

"Why not go to the apartment?"

His father had been in the process of lifting his drink, but his hand froze for a split second before he took a sip.

"Yeah," Reid said. "I know about the apartment. So does everyone else in the office. I'm sure Mother knows about it, too."

Something hard glittered in Boone's eyes as he polished off his drink and poured himself another. "I hear you sold your condo. Bought one of those old properties on Logan Street and opened an office. How's that working out for you?"

"It's early days, but I'm staying busy."

"I also hear you had a meeting with Clement Mayfair yesterday. Trying to land yourself a big one, are you?"

Reid frowned. "Where did you hear that?"

"You know how things work in this town. Small circles, big mouths." His father observed him for a moment. "A word of advice?"

"Why not?"

"Think twice before you get into bed with a guy like Clement Mayfair. He's as vicious and vindictive as they come. You cross a line with him, you make an enemy for life."

Reid thought about Clement Mayfair's earlier warning. "He told me he had dealings with you in the past. He called you overconfident and self-indulgent. To be fair, he said the same about me."

Boone smirked. "It's not overconfidence if you can deliver."

"No, I suppose not," Reid said. "You were his attorney?"

"About a hundred years ago."

"What happened?"

Boone made a dismissive gesture with his hand. "Nothing seismic. Your mother and I were good friends with Evelyn. When they separated, it created a conflict of interest."

"So you chose Evelyn."

"It really wasn't much of a choice. I was glad to see the last of Clement Mayfair."

Reid toyed with his glass. "Do you know why they split?"

His father gave him a curious look. "It didn't have anything to do with me if that's what you're implying. I thought the world of Evelyn. She was something back in her day, but I've never gone for older women."

Reid said drily, "Not everything is about you, you know."

"Just most things." Boone grinned.

Reid wasn't amused. "From what Arden has told me, the separation was anything but amicable. Evelyn took the daughter and Clement kept the son. Sounds like a pretty screwed-up arrangement if you ask me."

"The Mayfairs are a pretty screwed-up lot," Boone

said. "I don't say that to malign your girlfriend. I've always been fond of Arden."

"She's not my girlfriend."

The denial didn't seem to register. His father leaned an elbow on the marble countertop as he nursed his third drink. "Has Arden ever showed you the family photograph albums?"

"I guess. A long time ago."

"Have her show you again. Take a close look at the faces, the eyes. Arden is the spitting image of her mother, just as Camille was the mirror image of Evelyn. Calvin takes after the old man but with enough Berdeaux blood to soften the hard edges. Ask yourself why Calvin favors both his mother and father, but there is nothing of Clement Mayfair in either of the girls."

Reid stared at him across the counter. "Are you suggesting—"

"I'm not suggesting anything. It's merely an observation." Although Boone sounded sober enough, Reid wondered if his father had been drinking before he ever reached the kitchen door. There was a strange glitter in his eyes, as if he might be enjoying his disparagement of Clement Mayfair a little too much.

Reid thought about the implications of his father's observation. If Clement had found out that Camille wasn't his biological daughter, that would explain the acrimonious separation and the lingering bitterness. That would also explain why Evelyn was allowed to take Camille and forced to leave Calvin behind.

"Why are you so interested in Mayfair ancient history anyway?" his father asked.

"Arden thinks Clement may try to take Berdeaux Place away from her."

His father lifted a brow. "Is that so? Well, I can't say I'm surprised. He's always had a thing about that house. It represents everything he ever desired and could never attain. Legacy. Respectability. Acceptance."

"What are you talking about? Mayfair House is twice the size of Berdeaux Place, and it's been a part of the iconic imagery of Battery Row for generations."

"His grandfather..." Boone frowned. "Or was it his great-grandfather? No matter. Some dead Mayfair lost the house and most of the family money in a series of shady business deals. Another family lived in Mayfair House until Clement made his own fortune. He bought back the property and had money left to burn, but he still wasn't welcome in certain circles. Only his marriage to Evelyn opened those doors and he always resented her for it. After the divorce, he withdrew from society. Sent Calvin away to boarding school, and became reclusive and hostile. Lately, though, I've heard rumbles about efforts to rehabilitate his image. Maybe that has something to do with Arden. He is getting on in years. In any case, she's smart to be on guard."

Reid declined to point out that Clement Mayfair wasn't so much older than Boone. "You haven't heard anything brewing in regards to Berdeaux Place?"

"No, but I'll keep my ear to the ground. If I hear anything I'll let you know."

"Thanks. I appreciate that. Arden will, too."

His father tilted his head, regarding Reid through

bloodshot eyes. "This thing with you and Arden. It's just business these days?"

Reid lifted the glass and took his first sip, buying himself a moment. "I told her I'd ask around about her grandfather and, in turn, she's helping me on another case. One of your old clients, as a matter of fact. Dave Brody."

Boone paused just a fraction too long. "Who?"

"Dave Brody. He hasn't tried to contact you?"

"I'm a hard man to reach unless you have my cell number, and I don't give that out to just anybody."

"Brody was sent up on a second-degree murder conviction ten years ago. He got out of prison a few weeks ago and he's been following me around, watching my house. Making a general nuisance of himself."

Boone's face had grown tense and wary. "What does he want with you?"

"He wants me to find Ginger Vreeland." Reid saw the dart of a shadow across his father's expression. "I take it that name rings a bell?"

Boone lifted his drink. "What did he tell you?"

"He thinks you're the reason she left town the night before she was to take the witness stand on his behalf."

"What?"

Reid nodded. "He claims Ginger kept a little black book with all her clients' numbers and—shall we say—preferences? You were afraid of what she might reveal on the witness stand so you paid her to disappear."

"That's ludicrous." Boone slammed his glass to the marble counter so aggressively Reid wondered that the crystal didn't shatter. "Brody was a real piece of work even back then. Guilty as hell, but always wanting to blame his misfortune on someone else. I suggest you keep your distance. Take out a restraining order if you have to."

"I can't do that," Reid said. "He claims someone is trying to set me up for murder and he's the only one who can help clear me."

"Murder?" His father looked stunned. "What are you talking about?"

"You heard about the body that was found Monday morning in an alley down the street from my place? Turns out, the victim and I were in the same bar on the night she was killed. I don't remember her. I don't remember much of anything about that night, but Brody claims he has photographs of the two of us together. He'll take them to the police if I don't help him find Ginger Vreeland. A restraining order wouldn't stop him. It would only egg him on."

"Then just back off. Let me take care of Brody."

That was like him, Reid thought. Always thinking he knew best. Reid couldn't help but remember Brody's taunt about Boone Sutton swooping in to save the day. Or Arden's tentative speculation that his father could be behind everything.

"It's not that simple," Reid said. "One of the detectives on the case is a man named John Graham. He arrested me years ago for driving under the influence. He thinks you not only called in favors to get my record expunged, but you also meddled in his career. So you getting involved will only make things worse all the way around."

"I remember that cop," Boone said. "Bad temper. God complex. Guys like him give all the other police officers a bad name. If he had career setbacks, it was because of his incompetence and attitude. He'd already been suspended once for unreasonable force, by the way. Then he had those two inmates work you over. He should have been fired on the spot. No second chances."

"Why wasn't he?"

"My guess is someone with enough money and clout decided he could be useful. That's how this town works, too."

Was it you? Reid wondered. *Are you the reason John Graham still has a badge?*

"I'll talk to some people," Boone said.

"No, don't do that. All I want from you is Ginger Vreeland's address. Or at least her last known whereabouts."

"So you can try to bargain with Brody?" His father leaned in so close that Reid could follow the roadmap of those tiny red veins in his eyes. "Has it ever occurred to you that Ginger would have had more than one name in her book? More than one name, more than one secret. Her disappearance had nothing to do with me. Maybe she left town because she was afraid."

That stopped Reid cold. "Someone threatened her?"

Boone straightened. "I've said all I can say. You need to let this one go, Reid. Forget you ever heard the name Ginger Vreeland. You have no idea the can of worms you're trying to open."

Chapter Twelve

Arden was seated behind Reid's desk working on her laptop when he got back to the office that afternoon. Despite yesterday's experience, she barely glanced up when he came in the back door, she was that engrossed in the photographs.

"What a day I've had." He glanced in from the kitchen doorway. "You want a drink?"

She answered without looking up. "Thought you'd stopped drinking for now."

"I meant water or a Coke."

"No, I'm fine. I've had a day, too," she said, letting excitement creep into her voice. "You'll never believe what I have to show you."

She heard him close the fridge and then pop the tab on a soda. "So what are you working on?" he asked. "The website?"

"No, not yet. Right now, I'm going through some photographs." She finally glanced up. He stood in the archway leaning a shoulder against the door frame. He'd removed his coat and tie and rolled up his shirt-sleeves, revealing his tanned forearms. He looked tall and lean and handsome, the grown-up version of the boy she'd once loved beyond all reason. A thrill raced up her spine in spite of her best efforts. And with those tingles came a memory.

Don't be like that, Reid. Just say it.

Why do I need to say it? You know how I feel.

Because I need to hear it, that's why.

All right, then. I love you, Arden Mayfair. I've loved you from the moment I first laid eyes on you, and I'll love you until the moment I leave this earth. How's that?

"What photographs?" Reid asked.

"What?"

He nodded to the laptop. "You said you were going through some photographs."

"Oh. Right. The photos." She cleared her throat and glanced away. She was letting herself think too much about the past today, falling into the trap of all those old memories. She and Reid had known each other forever, and, yes, she'd once felt closer to him than anyone else on earth. But that was a long time ago. They were adults now with career setbacks and bills and a plethora of other problems that had to be dealt with before she could even think about the future.

"Arden?"

She cleared her throat again. "I want to show you something, but you have to promise you won't get upset."

"I already don't like the sound of that, so no." He pushed away from the door frame and ambled over to the desk, leaning against the edge as he gazed down at her. "I'm not making you any promises."

"Okay. Just keep in mind that I'm perfectly safe. Nothing happened."

"Arden." He drawled out her name. "What have you done?"

The intensity of his gaze…the way he tilted his head as he stared down at her…

She sighed. Even suspicious Reid was suddenly irresistible to her. Maybe it was that death thing she'd read about. *Someone dies and suddenly all you want to do is have sex so that you can feel alive.* She'd never personally experienced such a reaction. Maybe it wasn't even a real thing. Maybe she was just—

"What is going on with you?" Reid asked. "I've never seen you so distracted."

"I have a lot on my mind, as I'm sure you do." She brushed back her hair. "Maybe I should just show you the images and then we'll talk. Talk not yell," she added.

"We'll see."

He turned to lean in, placing a hand on the desk and another on the back of her chair. Too close. She couldn't breathe, so she rolled away slightly, hoping he wouldn't notice.

"What? Did my deodorant fail me or something?"

"You smell fine," she said with an inward cringe.

"You're acting really weird today."

"I know. Let's concentrate on the photographs." She clicked on the thumbnails to enlarge the images.

"Brody didn't lie. He really did take photos of you and the victim in that bar."

Reid leaned in even closer. "Where did you get these?"

"Someone emailed them to me."

He reached over and clicked another image. "Who?"

"I did," she admitted. "I emailed them to myself."

He turned with a frown. "Where did you get them?"

"They were on Dave Brody's laptop, which I found in his apartment after I broke in." She said it all in a rush.

"You *what*?"

"I didn't actually break in," she clarified. "I used a key that I found in a flowerpot."

He gave a quick shake of his head as if he couldn't keep up with her explanation. "Hold on. What key, what flowerpot?"

She gave him a mostly abbreviated version of events, but there was no way to sugarcoat her hiding in Brody's bathtub to avoid him.

Reid swiveled her chair around so that she couldn't avoid his gaze. "What were you thinking? Did you even consider what would happen if he caught you in his apartment?"

"But he didn't catch me. I'm perfectly fine. And I kept my head enough to wipe my fingerprints off the laptop before I left. He'll never know I was there."

"Did you wipe down the doorknobs? What about the key? Are you certain the landlady didn't see you enter or leave?" Reid looked to be hanging on to his cool by a thread. "Damn it, Arden. That could have gone wrong in so many ways. I don't even know what to say to you right now."

"How about, good job, Arden. How about, let's take a closer look at these photographs."

He wasn't amused. "How about, you put yourself needlessly at risk and proved that I can't trust you."

Arden was starting to get a little irritated. "You're making too big a deal of this."

"I've barely gotten started. We had an agreement, remember? My office, my firm, my rules."

"I wasn't in the office. I was on my lunch break. I would assume my free time is my own."

"Now you're just being deliberately willful."

"And you're being—what was the word you used the other night—pedestrian," she shot back. "When has either of us ever played by the rules? You actually followed Brody into a dark alley where a woman had been killed the night before. So don't tell me you wouldn't have done the same thing in my place."

"That's different."

"Oh, because you're a man and I'm a woman?"

"No, because this is my problem. I don't want you taking that kind of risk on my behalf."

"It's not just your problem and, for your information, I didn't do it just for you. I want to find out who killed Haley Cooper as much as you do. For all we know, I could be the next victim."

That seemed to take the wind out of his sails. "I won't let that happen."

"Unless we find out what's really going on, you may not be able to stop it. That's why I went up to

Brody's apartment. I hoped I could find evidence of the real killer's identity or, at the very least, whether or not someone is paying him to frame you. If you'd settle down for a minute and look at the photographs, I mean, *really look* at the photographs, you might find something interesting."

"Arden…"

"I don't want to fight about this anymore," she said.

"I don't want to fight, either. I was just about to say I'm sorry."

"For what?" she asked suspiciously.

His eyes glinted and a smile flickered. "For being too much like Boone Sutton."

"You're nothing like Boone Sutton. You never were."

His hands were still on the chair arms as he gazed into her eyes. Lips slightly parted. Heart starting to race. Or was that hers?

He leaned in, brushing his lips against hers and Arden's pulse jumped. It was a brief kiss, barely any contact at all, and yet she felt a tremor go straight through her, making her crave a deeper connection. She wanted to feel his tongue in her mouth and his hands on her breasts. She wanted him to whisk her upstairs and undress her slowly with the balcony doors open and the scent of jasmine drifting in on the breeze. She wanted time to melt away, but those fourteen years of estrangement were right there between them, creating obstacles and barriers that she didn't dare breach.

He moved his head away, just a few inches, and smiled down at her. "Sorry again."

"For what?"

"For being too much like the old Reid Sutton."

"Don't ever apologize for that. The old Reid Sutton was pretty wonderful."

"As opposed to the current Reid Sutton?"

"Time will tell," she teased.

For a moment, she thought he might accept the challenge and kiss her again, but he turned back to the laptop and the moment was gone.

Arden scooted back up to the desk and sorted through the photographs until she found the one she wanted, and then she magnified the image.

"What am I looking for?" Reid asked.

"Just study the picture and tell me what you see."

"It's pretty dark, but I recognize a couple of my friends in the background. There I am standing at the bar. The woman next to me is the victim, Haley Cooper. I know because Detective Graham showed me a picture of her. At least I think she's the same woman. It's hard to know for certain."

"Even in the dim lighting, certain faces stand out," Arden said. "Keep looking."

Reid frowned. "Why don't you just tell me who or what I'm looking for?"

"Check out the man at the end of the bar. His head is turned toward you, and he appears to be staring at either you or the victim or both."

Reid concentrated for a moment and slowly turned his head toward Arden. "Is that who I think it is?"

"Sure looks like him to me. What are the chances

that Detective Graham would be in that particular bar on that particular night?"

Reid focused on the photograph. "Are you sure it's him?"

"Not one hundred percent. As you said, the photograph is dark, but look at the hair, the way he holds his drink. The expression on his face. You can almost feel the contempt. I don't think his being there was a coincidence. My question is this. Why didn't he tell you that he'd seen you on the night Haley Cooper was murdered?"

"Maybe he wanted to catch me in a lie. Or see if I'd incriminate myself."

"Did you? Lie to him, I mean?"

"I told him she looked vaguely familiar. There was a chance I might have seen her around the neighborhood."

"And he didn't say or do anything to give himself away?"

"No, but I was concentrating pretty hard on not giving myself away. I might not have noticed."

"I did some digging while you were out," Arden said. "There's a lot of information on the internet about cops if you know where to look. Detective Graham has a pretty checkered history with the Charleston PD. Suspensions. Internal Affairs investigations. And that's not all. His personal life is a mess, too. He's going through a second bad divorce. Lots of debt. That kind of guy could be bought off."

Reid gave her an admiring look. "Where did you find all this stuff?"

"Blogs, message boards, news sites. A person's whole life is online." She paused. "Do you think he could be the one who came into your house yesterday?"

"You tell me. You saw him on the porch. Could he have been the intruder?"

She thought about that for a moment. "He's the right size and height, but I never got a look at the man's face. I figured Dave Brody. Regardless, how did the intruder get a key?"

"Maybe he found it in a flowerpot," Reid deadpanned.

She made a face. "Or maybe he got it from the real estate agent who sold you this house. He could have spun any kind of story to get the agent to cooperate. What about motive, though? I get that he doesn't like rich people, but it's hard to believe he'd nurse a grudge against you personally. All because your father got you out of jail?"

"He also thinks Boone meddled in his career. Don't forget that part. And speaking of the devil…" Reid went around the desk and sat down in one of the client chairs. "I saw him today."

"Your father? You went to his office?"

"No, I went by the house. I thought Mother and the housekeeper would be out and I could search his office. See if I could find anything that connects him to Ginger Vreeland."

"Did you?"

"He came home before I had a chance to look around. I told him I was there to see Mother, but I don't think he believed me. Luckily, he was too preoccupied—and possibly inebriated—to press me.

Anyway, I brought up Brody's name. He pretended he didn't know who he was until I mentioned Ginger Vreeland. Then he became visibly distressed and implied that she'd left town because one of her clients had threatened her."

"Did he say who?"

"No, but he was pretty adamant that I leave Ginger alone. He told me in no uncertain terms that I should walk away."

"You're not going to, are you?"

Reid's gaze hardened. "How can I as long as Brody has leverage over me?"

"Then should I move forward with the website and business cards? The sooner we contact her uncle, the closer we are to finding Ginger."

"Yes, go ahead, and make sure you run everything by me before you do anything else. In other words, don't go off on your own trying to track this guy down."

"You have my word." Arden closed the laptop and began gathering up her things. "It's been a long day. I'm heading home now. I've been so distracted by everything that's happened here, I'm behind on the things I need to do at Berdeaux Place."

"Whenever you're ready, I'll drive you," Reid said.

Arden stood and hooked her bag over her shoulder. "That's not necessary. I enjoy the walk. Gives me a chance to get reacquainted with the city."

Reid rose, too. "You'll have plenty of time for that later. It's a long walk and it'll be twilight soon. I don't want you out on the street with Brody lurking around.

Before you argue—it has nothing to do with your gender," he said. "It's just common sense."

Hard to disagree with that. Arden nodded. "You're right. We both need to take precautions these days. A ride would be great."

They walked out the back door, pausing on the porch for Reid to lock up. Then they went down the steps together and crossed the yard to the driveway. Arden took a moment to admire the sleek lines of his car before she climbed inside and settled comfortably onto the seat. She ran a hand over the padded leather as Reid started the engine.

"Nice ride. But it kind of stands out in this neighborhood, don't you think?"

He grinned. "Why do you think I park around back? I thought about selling it when I got rid of the condo. I could have used the extra cash, but I'm a Southern boy born and bred. When it comes right down to it, I'd sooner cut off my right arm than get rid of my wheels."

"I sold my car before I left Atlanta," Arden said. "I sold or gave away everything except whatever I could pack in my bags."

Reid shot her a glance. "Clean break."

"Yeah."

They were out on the street now heading toward the tip of the peninsula. Reid checked the rearview mirror and then checked it again.

"What is it?" she asked anxiously.

"Probably nothing. A beige sedan has been behind us for a few blocks. No, don't turn around," he said.

Arden looked in the outside mirror. "Two cars back?

Do you think it could be Graham? Looks like an unmarked cop car."

"Let's find out." Reid gave her a warning glance. "You better hold on!"

Chapter Thirteen

Reid jerked the wheel, executing a sharp right turn at the last minute. Then he goosed the accelerator for half a block, threw on the brakes and reversed into an alley.

Through all the maneuvers, Arden clung to the armrest and the edge of her seat. When he finally came to a full stop, she released her held breath. "Are you insane? You nearly gave me a heart attack back there."

"I did warn you to hold on." He focused his gaze on the street in front of them. "Anyway, that's just adrenaline. Don't pretend you didn't like it."

"Maybe I did," she conceded. "That doesn't make you any less crazy."

"No, but it does give me back my partner in crime."

"I don't know if I would go that far." Arden tried not to react to his words. She told herself they meant nothing. It was a slip of the tongue in the heat of the moment. But adrenaline buzzed through her veins. "Where did you learn to drive like that anyway?"

Another grin flashed. "Just a God-given talent. I'm surprised you didn't remember that about me."

"Maybe I tried to forget." Arden faced forward,

watching the street. "Do you think we lost him? That is, if anyone was following us in the first place."

"We'll sit here for a minute or two and make sure." Reid seemed to relax as time ticked away. He rolled down his windows so they could hear the sounds from the street. The smell of barbecue and fresh bread drifted in. "You hungry? We could stop somewhere for a bite to eat."

Arden was starving, as a matter of fact, and it would be so easy to take Reid up on his offer. Drift right back into the comfortable relationship of their youth. Have some wine, some food, some good conversation. She couldn't think of a more pleasant way to spend the evening, but rushing things was a very bad idea. They were still building a work rapport and for now a little personal distance was necessary. *Just wait and see how things play out.* She didn't have the stamina for a broken heart. "I appreciate the offer, but I'm beat. Another time?"

He nodded. "Yeah, no problem. I could use an early night myself." He eased out of the alley and melded into the late-afternoon traffic. Keeping an eye on the rearview mirror, he maneuvered effortlessly through the clogged streets, pulling to the curb in front of Berdeaux Place within a matter of minutes.

Arden reached for the door handle. "You don't need to get out," she said when he killed the engine. "I changed the security code so that even if anyone used a key to get in, they'd set off the alarm. I would have been notified if there'd been a breach." Brave words, but the truth of the matter was that Arden dreaded going inside the empty house. Feared another long night of sounds and shadows and dark memories.

"I'll come in and take a quick look around. For my own peace of mind." He reached across her and removed a small pistol from the glove box.

Arden gasped. "Reid. What are you doing with a gun?"

"I have a license, don't worry."

"That doesn't answer my question."

"Lawyers make enemies," he said as he tucked the gun into the back of his belt.

"You mean like Brody?"

"He or someone else came into my house while you were there alone. I don't intend to be caught off guard again."

Arden started to protest—guns scared her—but who was she to cast stones? Hadn't she slept with her grandmother's katana the night before?

They got out of the car and walked up the veranda steps together. She unlocked the door, turned off the alarm and trailed Reid through the house as he went from room to room. Then she led the way upstairs. She refused to go inside her mother's room. She leaned a shoulder against the wall and waved toward the door. "I'll wait out here for you."

While he was inside, she hollered through the doorway. "See anything?"

"Nope, all clear in here."

"Smell anything?"

There was a significant pause. "Like what?"

"Nothing. I just wondered."

He came out into the hallway and gave her a puzzled look. "What was that about?"

"I heard something last night. I went into my mother's room to check things out and I noticed a magnolia-scented candle on her dresser. For a split second, I had the crazy notion that someone had been inside her room burning that candle."

Reid frowned down at her. "You told me you were kept awake by squirrels."

"A scrabbling sound brought me upstairs, and yes, it probably was just squirrels. Or worse, rats." She shuddered. "I told you this morning. Being in this house is a lot more unnerving than I thought it would be."

"Then move into a hotel for the time being. It would certainly make me feel better."

"I can't afford that right now and, besides, I don't want to. I don't want to become that person who's afraid of her own shadow. I'll take the necessary precautions, but I'm not going to be forced out of my own home. I'm sure that's just what my grandfather would like to happen."

"Stubborn as always."

"I prefer to think of myself as determined."

Reid checked the second-floor bedrooms and took a peek in the attic. Satisfied that everything was as it should be, they went back downstairs. He paused in the doorway of the parlor to glance out into the garden. "You think your uncle is working in the greenhouse?"

"I doubt it. I saw him earlier today. He gave me back the key to the side gate. He'd have to crawl over the wall like you did to get inside."

"Assuming he didn't make himself a spare key," Reid said.

"Why would he do that? Why not just keep the original key? I never asked for it back."

"Maybe he thought you would eventually. I'm just thinking out loud." Reid went over and opened one of the doors, letting in the late-afternoon breeze. He moved out into the garden and Arden followed reluctantly. If the house unnerved her, the garden put her even more on edge, especially when the sun went down and the bats came out.

She folded her arms around her middle. "I saw him today. My uncle Calvin. He gave me a portrait he'd painted of my mother. He said he worked from a picture of her that was taken here in the garden on the night of the Mayor's Ball. I remember the dress she wore that night. Red chiffon. It floated like a dream around her when she walked. And she'd tucked a magnolia blossom in her hair." Arden paused, suddenly drowning in memories. "You can't imagine how beautiful she looked."

"I think I have some idea," Reid murmured. "Some people think you're the spitting image of Camille."

"A pale copy, maybe." His gaze on her was a little too intense so Arden made a production of plucking a sprig of jasmine and holding it to her nose. "Should we check the greenhouse while we're out here? I don't think my uncle came by, but I'd like to make sure the door is secure. The latch sometimes doesn't catch and I'd rather not have the wind bumping it at all hours..." She trailed off, letting the jasmine drop to her feet as she stared up into the trees. The light shimmering down through the leaves was already starting to wane. Twilight would soon fall and then darkness. She pictured the shadowy sidewalks outside the walls of Berdeaux Place and shivered. "Do you remember how it was that summer?" she asked.

"The summer your mother died?"

"Yes, I mean afterward, when we started hearing about the other victims. No one ever talked about the Twilight Killer in front of me, of course, but I overheard just enough to be terrified. I used to wake up in the middle of the night and think that I could hear his heartbeat in my room. I imagined him underneath my bed or hiding in my closet. Sometimes I would get up and go over to the window just to make sure he wasn't down in the garden staring up at my window."

"It was a very dark time in this city."

"Reid, what if we were right all those years ago?" Arden turned to him in the failing light. He stood in shadows, his features dark and mysterious and yet becoming once again as familiar to her as her own reflection. "What if the person who murdered all those women, including my mother, is still out there somewhere? The real Twilight Killer. Maybe he's taken more lives over the years, even before Haley Cooper. He could have broadened his hunting ground and spread out his kills so that the police never connected his victims. An animal with those kinds of cravings can't remain dormant forever. If he is still out there, then he framed an innocent man once. Maybe his impulses are growing stronger and he feels another spree coming on so he needs another scapegoat. He started seeding the ground with Haley."

"By scapegoat, you mean me?"

"That's what worries me," she said.

Reid didn't chide her for letting her imagination get the better of her as she thought he might. Instead, he let his gaze travel over the grounds, settling his focus on the summerhouse dome. "Assuming Orson Lee Finch really is innocent, he made the perfect patsy. Nearly invisible and moving at will in and out of the gardens South of Broad Street. Plenty of opportunities to observe and follow his victims. And once arrested, he had to rely on a public defender. No money, no friends, no family to speak of." He turned back to Arden. "I'm not Finch. I have access to the finest defense team in the city, not to mention a plethora of private detectives. I'm hardly powerless, so you have to ask yourself why a spree killer would want to try and frame someone with my resources. That doesn't make sense."

"Unless you're not even the real target. Maybe I am." Arden shivered. With the setting sun, a stronger breeze blew in from the harbor, carrying the faintest trace of pluff mud through the trees. Her grandmother used to call that particular aroma the perfume of rumors and old scandal. The fecund smell was there one moment, gone the next, replaced by the ubiquitous scent of jasmine.

"Maybe we're overthinking this," Reid said. "Trying to connect everything back to the Twilight Killer is making us overlook the revenge angle. Maybe this is nothing more than a simple frame job. A way to get to my father because Brody can't touch him."

"So Detective Graham being in the bar the night of the murder was just a coincidence?"

"I don't know what to think about Graham." The breeze ruffled Reid's hair, making Arden long to run her fingers through the mussed strands. "I need to tell you something else about my conversation with Boone today."

His tone made her breath catch. "What?"

"He suggested that we should take a look at your family photo albums."

"Why?" she asked in surprise.

"He thinks Clement Mayfair might not have been your mother's biological father."

Arden whirled. "What?"

"You've never considered the possibility?" Reid asked. "You never heard any talk to that effect?"

"Not a word. But…" She trailed off as her mind went back through those photo albums. So many portraits and candid shots of Arden and her mother and grandmother, fewer of Calvin, and none at all of her grandfather. Hardly surprising considering the lingering animosity. "If I'm honest, I can't say that would surprise me. It makes a sick kind of sense, doesn't it? Why Grandmother took my mother and left Calvin behind with my grandfather? He probably threatened to take both her children away from her."

"Has he made contact?"

"No. But I'm more certain than ever that his real

interest is in acquiring this house. He doesn't care anything about me. He never did."

"His loss," Reid said.

Arden shrugged. "I'm sure he doesn't see it that way. I think I should go see him. I know you advised against it, but I want to make it clear that I'm not afraid of him and that he is never going to get his hands on Grandmother's house."

"Just hold off for a bit," Reid said. "Everything we've talked about is pure speculation. There's no point in antagonizing him until he makes a move. It's possible that he really does want to make amends."

"I'll wait. But not forever." Arden turned to make her way to the greenhouse. Reid had stopped on the path and was staring in the opposite direction. "What's wrong?"

"Let's check out the summerhouse first." He nodded toward the ornate dome. "We're right here and I'd like to see how it's held up over the years."

"I'd rather not. I don't like going inside," Arden admitted.

"Since when? You used to love the summerhouse. It was our place."

"It was his place first," she said.

He gave her a bemused look. "Are you talking about your mother's killer? There was never any evidence that he hid inside."

"The magnolia blossom on the steps would suggest otherwise."

"Okay, but that was a long time ago, and you and

I made this place our headquarters for years. Why so reticent now?"

"I can't explain it," Arden said. "It just feels... wrong. Evil."

"It's just a place. A beautiful old summerhouse. You've been away too long. You've forgotten the good things that happened inside. Maybe a quick look around is all you need to put the ghosts to rest. You may find the good memories outweigh the bad."

Maybe that's what I'm really afraid of.

Nevertheless, she followed him up the steps and into the summerhouse. The latticework windows cast mysterious shadows on the floor while twilight edged toward the domed ceiling. Arden turned in a slow circle. The pillows that had cushioned their heads as they'd lain on their backs staring up at the stars were gone, along with all their treasures. The place smelled of dust and decay. But some things remained. Somewhere on the wall were their carved initials; Arden didn't want to look too closely. She didn't want to remember how much she'd given up when she left Charleston fourteen years ago.

"It's a little the worse for wear," Reid said as he moved around the space. "But it does bring back memories."

"Our first grown-up kiss was here," she murmured. "Do you remember?"

"Of course, I remember."

She turned at the tenderness in his voice. Tenderness...and something more. Something darker and headier. Desire. Throbbing just below the surface. Not so strange, she supposed, that they would both feel strong emotions in this place.

"I kissed you and then you ran away," he said. "It was quite a blow to my ego."

"I was afraid."

"Of me?"

"Of what it meant. I knew after that kiss that nothing would ever be the same. I was afraid of losing my best friend."

His voice lowered intimately. "You didn't lose me."

"Easy to say. Not so easy to believe after fourteen years."

"I've always been right here, Arden." He slid his fingers into her hair, tilting her head so that he could stare down at her. "See?" he said. "There's nothing to be afraid of in here."

Arden wasn't so sure. She parted her lips, waiting to see what he would do.

Into the quivering silence came a distant sound, a rhythmic thumping that she could have easily believed was her own heartbeat.

Reid glanced toward the door as his hand fell to his side. "Did you hear that?"

She turned to peer out into the garden. "It's coming from the greenhouse. The wind is rising. It must have caught the door."

Reid was all business now. "We'd better go have a look."

They hurried down the steps together and Arden was overly conscious of Reid beside her, of the memories that still swirled in the ether as they approached the greenhouse. Enough daylight remained so that they could see inside the glass walls. Arden was once again reminded of her uncle's paintings and the feeling his art had evoked of being on the outside looking in.

She gazed down the empty aisles toward the back of the greenhouse, where she could see the silhouette of her mother's cereus. "I should check the progress while we're here. I don't want to risk missing the blooms and that luscious scent." *Like moonlight and romance and deep, dark secrets*, her mother would say.

"Arden, wait," Reid said as she stepped through the door.

"It's fine. There's no one here. Come have a closer look."

She was well down the aisle when she heard a loud crack above her and glanced up a split second before Reid grabbed her from behind. They dropped to the ground and instinctively rolled beneath one of the worktables. Arden tucked her legs and wrapped her arms around her head as Reid covered her body with his. She heard a series of pops as one of the heavy panels gave way and crashed to the stone floor beside them. The tempered glass exploded into harmless chips, but the weight of the panel would have crushed anyone standing in the aisle.

Chapter Fourteen

A structural issue—that was the consensus of the inspectors Arden hired to check out the greenhouse. Over the years, some of the clips that held the glass panels in place had come loose or fallen off altogether and the elements had eroded the silicone sealant. Add in a rusted frame, and the roof panels had been one stray breeze away from disaster for years. Everything pointed to coincidence, and Arden told herself she should just be thankful no one had been hurt. Still, she couldn't stop the little voice in her head that whispered of sabotage.

Before the greenhouse was disassembled and carted away, she had workers move her mother's cereus to the terrace. She liked that location better anyway. Now she could watch the blooms open from the safety of a locked door if she so chose.

Her return to Charleston had been harrowing, to say the least. Luckily, she knew how to tuck and roll and keep her head down. She spent a lot of time at work, burying herself in research and planning. Reid had outside meetings almost every day so she spent hours alone in his house. The solitude never bothered her, which was strange since she could barely spend one night alone in Berdeaux Place without succumbing to her dark imagination. She hadn't experienced any more strange sounds or scents, but every now and then her gaze would stray to her mother's bedroom door and she would wonder again if someone had been inside burning that magnolia-scented candle.

By Friday, the website had gone live, the business cards were printed, and everything was in place to approach Ginger Vreeland's uncle—a retired welder named Tate Smith—about her whereabouts.

She and Reid made the trek down south into marsh country together. The drive was pleasant, the day crystal clear, but the results of their search proved frustrating. Although Arden had searched public records for the last known address, the house appeared abandoned, as if no one had lived there in months, if not years. No one answered the door and none of the neighbors claimed to know Tate Smith or his niece. Arden wondered if Mr. Smith had been that reclusive or if the neighbors were simply protecting his privacy. She clipped a business card to a hastily scribbled message and slipped it underneath his door. Then she and Reid headed back to the city.

The weekend passed without further incident, but Arden couldn't relax. She worked in the office for a little while on Saturday morning and then went home to finish the list of everything that needed to be done to Berdeaux Place. Obviously, with the greenhouse failure, things were direr than she'd anticipated. As she explored the premises and grounds, she kept an eye out for her uncle so that she could explain what had happened. He never turned up. Dave Brody had vanished, as well. The deadline he'd set for Reid had come and gone, but for the moment, he seemed intent on keeping a low profile. Or else he'd gotten a message from Boone Sutton. No Dave Brody, no Detective Graham. No word from her grandfather, either.

Still, Arden knew better than to let down her guard, and as the days wore on, a pall seemed to settle over the city. An encroaching gloom that portended dark days ahead. She wanted to believe that Haley Cooper's murder had been random, a victim caught in the wrong place at the wrong time, but she had a feeling nothing about the woman's death or the killer's agenda was random. She now had an inkling of what Charleston had experienced during the Twilight Killer's reign of terror. The waiting. The imagined sounds. The impulse to hurry home before sundown and sequester oneself behind locked doors as shadows lengthened and dogs howled behind neighbors' fences.

She feared this quiet time might be the calm before the storm.

Another worry began to niggle. Reid had said nothing about extending her assignment, much less making the arrangement permanent. She hated to think of their time coming to an end. They'd settled into an amiable working relationship and Arden loved having a place to go to every morning. She admired his long-term plans for the firm, and, more than anything, she wanted to contribute to the success of those plans. But she refused to press him for an answer. His firm, his call.

Since the greenhouse incident, he'd kept things casual and that was a very good thing, Arden decided. The easy camaraderie had given them a chance to become friends again. Perhaps not the best buddies of their childhood—not yet—but the tension lessened with each passing day.

Or so she'd thought.

One afternoon she looked up from her work to find Reid standing in the doorway watching her with a puzzled expression, as if he couldn't quite figure her out. The intensity of his gaze caught her by surprise and her heart thudded, though she tried to keep her tone light.

"Everything okay?"

He folded his arms and leaned a shoulder against the door frame. He didn't have outside meetings that day and was dressed casually in jeans and a dark gray shirt open at the neck. "Do you ever wonder what our lives would be like now if things had worked out differently fourteen years ago?"

The question took Arden by surprise. She pretended to write herself a note while she pondered an answer. "I think about it sometimes, but I try not to dwell. We can't change the past." She shrugged. "Why bring it up now? I thought we'd moved past all that. We're working well together, aren't we?"

"We are," he agreed. "But don't you ever get the feeling we have unfinished business between us?"

Her heart knocked even harder against her rib cage. "What do you mean?"

He shifted his gaze to the window, frowning into the sunlight that streamed through the glass. "I've always wondered why you left the way you did. Why you barely even took the time to say goodbye. We were so close and after everything we'd been through, ending things the way we did felt...wrong."

"I thought it was better to get it over with quickly. Rip the bandage off and all that." She paused thoughtfully. "You always make it sound as if my leaving came out of the blue, but you know that's not the way it happened. We agreed that time apart would be good for us. Separate colleges gave us a chance to be independent. We were so young, and we had so much growing up to do. Maybe things worked out for the best. What's the point in looking back?"

He came into the office and sat down in a chair facing her desk. "It's not healthy to leave issues to fester."

"What issues?"

"All those times you were in Charleston for holidays and summer break. You *visited*, but you never really came back. You were here physically, but your mind and your heart were a million miles away. It was like you couldn't even stand the sight of me anymore. Like you hated me for what happened."

How would you know? Arden wanted to lash out. *You all but ignored me when I came home. You made me think there was nothing left for me here.*

Instead, she said, "That's what you thought? I didn't hate you. I never could. It was just hard for me to be here after everything that had happened. I felt so guilty. If only I'd taken better care of myself. If only I'd gone to the doctor sooner, if only I'd gotten more rest. And I felt even guiltier because a part of me was relieved when it happened. I know how awful that sounds, but it's the truth. That guilt is why I couldn't look at you."

"What happened wasn't your fault," he said.

"I know that. I probably knew it then, too, but my emotions were so fragile and everything between us seemed to be falling apart. We wanted different things, and that was never more apparent than in the way we each coped with our pain. You took comfort in the familiar. You wanted to cling to what we had. I wanted to run away. Maybe I should have tried harder to explain my feelings to you, but I probably didn't even understand them myself back then. I just knew I needed to get away from my grandmother's house."

"And from me."

"Yes, if I'm honest. We'd been inseparable since childhood. I needed a fresh start. I wanted to meet new people, have new adventures."

"I always thought we would have those adventures together," he said. "I didn't see why a baby had to stop us. I was young and stupid, and I had some crazy, romantic notion of how it could be, the three of us taking on the world. I never took into account what you would be giving up for my dream."

"As long as we're getting everything out in the open, I've always wondered why you never came to find me," she said. "In all those years, not a single phone call, email or text."

"You wanted your space."

"I thought I did." She shrugged. "Things don't always work out the way we want them to."

"And sometimes they work out in the way we least

expect." He held her gaze for the longest moment before he rose to leave.

"Reid?"

He glanced over his shoulder.

"Thank you for what you said just now. That it wasn't my fault."

"It wasn't. I should have told you a long time ago."

"You did. You told me over and over. I just wasn't ready to listen. Anyway…it's good to clear the air."

"Yeah."

He went back to his office without further comment.

Arden sat quietly for a few minutes and then got up to follow him. She said from his doorway, "Can I ask you something else? It's not about the past. Actually, it's more of a favor than a question."

He set aside his phone. "Should I be worried?"

"No, it's not like that." She pulled a creamy envelope from her dress pocket and walked over to slide it across his desk.

He picked up the envelope and glanced at the address. "What's this?"

"An invitation to the Mayor's Ball. It was delivered to Berdeaux Place earlier this week."

He glanced up. "That's cutting it a little close. Isn't the ball tomorrow night?"

"I was obviously a late addition to the guest list," she said. "I assume you got your invitation weeks ago."

He didn't seem the least bit interested. "I remember seeing one in the mail. Probably still around here somewhere."

"You weren't planning on going?"

He leaned back in his chair with a broad smile, the seriousness of their earlier conversation forgotten. "That's one of the perks of having my own firm. I no longer have to climb into a monkey suit to please my old man."

Arden sat down in the chair across from his desk, reversing their roles. "Did you happen to notice that it's being held at Mayfair House this year?"

He gave her a curious look. "How do you feel about that?"

"It's very strange. I never remember my grandfather having so much as a dinner party. He hated anyone, including me, intruding on his privacy, and now, suddenly, he's throwing open his doors to half of Charleston."

"My father said he'd heard rumblings about the old man trying to rehabilitate his image. He thought it might be for your benefit."

Arden shrugged. "I don't see how it could be. This had to be in the planning for months. Still, if I didn't suspect he was up to something before, I certainly do now."

"You really don't trust him, do you? Are you sure you aren't letting your grandmother's animosity cloud your judgment?"

She gave him an incredulous look. "You're asking me that after the conversation you had with him last week? Aren't you the one who told me to stay away from him?"

He leaned forward, his expression suspicious. "Yes, I did. Which is why I'm hoping you aren't planning to go to this thing tomorrow night."

She plucked at an invisible thread on her dress. "Of course, I'm going. It's the perfect place to interact with him for the first time. If I'm lucky, I may get some insight into what he's up to."

"Assuming he does have an agenda, he won't give himself away that easily," Reid warned. "Mayfair Place will be packed. Lots of press, lots of cameras. He'll be on his best behavior."

"Unless he's caught off guard."

"Arden." He drawled her name in that way he had. "What are you up to?"

"Nothing," she said innocently. "I just want to talk to him. And if you're really concerned about my safety, you'll go with me."

His eyes glinted, reminding her of the old Reid Sutton. "As your date?"

She hesitated. "As my friend or my boss. Whatever makes you feel most comfortable."

"Nothing about the Mayor's Ball makes me comfortable."

"Because you're looking at it all wrong," Arden insisted. "This is no longer about your father. This is about you and the future of your firm. Think about the guest list. Word will already have gotten around about Ambrose Foucault's imminent retirement. His clients will be there, ripe for the picking."

"I thought I wasn't allowed to go after his clients until his retirement is official," Reid said.

Arden tucked back her hair. "That was before he shared a private conversation with my uncle and possibly my grandfather. All bets are off now. As far as

I'm concerned, anyone who comes to that ball is fair game. Think of it as a scouting expedition. I may be a little rusty, but I daresay I can still work a room. And we both know you can charm birds out of a tree when you set your mind to it."

"Listen to you being all cutthroat."

She met his gaze straight on. "No, I'm being practical. A few of those old-money clients could help subsidize the other cases we want to take on." *You. The other cases* you *want to take on.* She started to correct herself, then decided changing the pronoun would call too much attention to her slip. Instead, she rushed to add, "If I haven't convinced you yet, then imagine all those wagging tongues when we walk into Mayfair House together."

He tapped the corner of the envelope on his desk. "I'll think about it."

She pounced. "What's there to think about? You know I'm right. I assume you still have a tux?"

"Buried in the back of my closet, where I like it."

"Dig it out for just this one night. And I'll wear something appropriately provocative."

"I'm almost afraid to ask what that means."

She merely smiled. "The invitation says eight. We'll arrive no earlier than nine thirty. Parking will be a nightmare, so leave your car at my house and we'll walk over together. It'll be so much easier than dealing with the valet service."

"You've got this all planned out, I see."

"Yes. All you have to do is show up on time." She stood to leave.

"Arden?"

She paused at the door.

"This surprise you're planning for your grandfather... You're not going to catch me off guard, too, are you?"

"You worry too much. It'll be a fun night. You'll see."

"Famous last words," he muttered.

ARDEN SPENT SATURDAY morning running errands. She picked up her dress at the dry cleaners and then dropped off her favorite necklace at a jewelry shop to have the clasp replaced. While she waited for the repair, she window-shopped along King Street, browsing some of the high-end boutiques to kill time. A crystal-studded belt in a window caught her eye, and she wandered in to check the price. A candle flickered on the counter next to the photograph of a young blonde woman whom Arden recognized as Haley Cooper.

The smiling countenance of the murder victim shocked her. She couldn't seem to get away from the horror. Then she remembered reading somewhere that Haley Cooper had worked in a shop on King Street.

She found the belt and decided the accessory would go so well with her gown that the splurge would be worth it. Plus, the purchase gave her the opportunity to speak with the woman behind the counter. As she rang up the item, Arden nodded to the photograph. "That's Haley, isn't it?"

The woman glanced up in surprise. "Did you know her?"

"No. I just recognize her photo from the news."

The woman gave her a grim smile. "At least you called her by name. Most of the people who comment on the photo ask if she's the dead woman. It's so impersonal to them. Just a news item or a crime statistic. They forget that Haley was a human being with friends and family who still miss her terribly." She bit her lip. "I'm so sorry. I don't know why I dumped all that on you. The last two weeks have been difficult."

"No apology necessary. Sometimes it's easier to talk to a stranger," Arden said with genuine sympathy. "Were the two of you close?"

"We became good friends after she started working here last year. She had a great personality. Funny. Smart. She was good with the customers, too." The woman hesitated, as if she wanted to resist but needed to get it all out. She busied her hands with tissue paper. "I know it must seem macabre that I have her photograph on display, but it's my shop. I can do what I want."

"Of course. And I don't think it's macabre at all," Arden said. "You're paying tribute to your friend."

"Yes, that. And I also promised myself I'd keep that candle burning until her killer is brought to justice. But, after two weeks, I'm starting to lose hope."

"I understand better than you think," Arden said. "My mother was murdered. Months went by before an arrest was made. I was young, but I remember the toll it took on my grandmother."

The woman's voice softened. "I'm so sorry. What a terrible thing to have happen to you."

Arden nodded. "It was a long time ago. But you don't forget." She paused. "Do you know if the police have any suspects?"

The woman carefully folded the tissue paper around the belt and secured it with a gold-embossed sticker. "They have *a* suspect. Who knows if anything will come of it?"

Arden tried to keep her tone soothingly neutral. "Do you know who it is?"

The woman took a quick perusal of the shop. A sales associate was busy with another customer at the clearance rack, too far away to overhear. The owner dropped her voice anyway. "You know what they say. It's always the spouse or boyfriend."

Arden lifted a brow. "Haley was seeing someone?"

"Yes. I never met him and she wouldn't say much about him. I had the impression he was an older man with money. That would have impressed Haley. She liked nice things."

"She never mentioned a name?"

"She was always careful not to let anything slip. She said he would be very upset if he knew she had mentioned him at all. He guarded his privacy. That didn't always sit well with Haley. She was young and she liked to go out. She wanted to be wined and dined."

"I heard on the news that she'd gone out to meet someone on the night of the murder. Do you think she met this man?"

The woman shrugged. "It's possible. But I know

they had a falling-out a few days before it happened. Haley was seeing someone on the side, but I never got the impression it was romantic. If anything, I think she was trying to spite the older guy."

"Then that would make two suspects," Arden said.

The owner looked as if she wanted to comment further, but three young women came into the shop talking and laughing and drawing her attention. She placed the belt and receipt in a glossy black bag and handed Arden the purchase.

"Enjoy the belt. I'm sure it will look lovely on you."

"Thank you."

Arden walked out of the boutique and glanced around. Her uncle's studio was just up the block. She wondered if she should stop by and warn him about the greenhouse. No, he was probably busy and she'd be seeing him later that night anyway. She realized she was avoiding him and she wasn't sure why. He'd been nothing but cordial and welcoming, and yet she sensed that he, too, had an ulterior motive for his interest in her.

Her phone rang as she walked back toward the jewelry store. She fished it out of her bag and then realized the ringtone belonged to the burner phone she'd purchased for contacting Ginger Vreeland. She didn't recognize the incoming number. Lifting the phone to her ear, she said crisply, "Arden Mayfair."

Silence.

"Hello? Anyone there?"

A female voice said anxiously, "I hear you've been looking for me."

Arden's pulse jumped. "Is this Ginger?"

"Don't say that name."

"Sorry." Arden backed up against the building so that she didn't block pedestrian traffic. "You got my message?"

"What do you want?" The woman's Low Country drawl was deep and hardened by suspicion and hostility.

"As I tried to explain in my note, we need to see you in person so that—"

"You think I don't recognize a con when I hear one? There's no bank, there's no money and I seriously doubt you're an attorney. You have five seconds to tell me what you really want."

"I just want to talk."

"What about?"

"Did you know Dave Brody is out of prison?"

A brief pause. "So? What's that to do with you?"

"I work for an attorney named Reid Sutton. I'm sure you recognize his name. Brody is threatening to make life unpleasant for a lot of people if we don't get him what he wants."

"Which is?"

"He thinks someone paid you to leave town before you could testify on his behalf, and he wants to know who and why. Personally, I think you were threatened. I think you left town because you were afraid."

A longer pause. "You don't know anything about me. If you're smart, you'll keep it that way."

Arden's pulse quickened. She'd hit a nerve. "We

can help you. Just name a time and place and we'll come meet you."

"That's not going to happen."

"Why not?"

"Did you really think he'd stop at one?"

The hair prickled at the back of Arden's neck. Phone still to her ear, she turned to glance over her shoulder, scouring the street behind her. "What do you mean?"

"The body that was found in the alley," Ginger said. "She wasn't his first victim. If you're not careful, she won't be his last."

"If you know who he is—"

"Just leave me alone, okay? I can take care of myself. And whatever you do, don't contact my uncle again. If anything happens to him, his blood will be on your hands."

Arden could hear traffic noises over the phone before the connection dropped. She positioned her body so that she could watch the sidewalk in both directions. No one looked suspicious. No one stared at her for an unseemly amount of time. That made no difference. Her every instinct warned of danger.

Somewhere close by, a coiled snake lay in wait.

Chapter Fifteen

Reid found himself surprisingly nervous when he arrived at Berdeaux Place that night. He told himself he was being ridiculous. Arden had gone out of her way to clarify that she didn't consider this a date. He was escorting her to the Mayor's Ball as a friend or her boss. *Whatever makes you feel more comfortable.*

He tugged at his bow tie as she buzzed him in through the gate. He parked, locked his car and then headed across the side lawn to the garden doors. She whisked them open and stepped out onto the patio, backlit by the lamplight spilling out from the parlor.

Reid froze, his breath escaping in a long, slow whistle as he took her in.

She spun so that the airy fabric of her gown caught the breeze. The scent of jasmine deepened in the dark, and the moon rising over the treetops cast the garden in a misty glow. The night suddenly seemed surreal to Reid, as though he were remembering a dream.

He shook his head slightly as if to clear his senses. "That dress..."

She lifted the frothy fabric. "Do you like it?"

"You look… Well, I suspect you already know how you look." Her hair fell in gleaming waves about her bare shoulders, and when she moved, moonlight sparked off the diamond studs in her earlobes and the crystal belt she wore around her waist.

"It was my mother's," she said. "I found it in my grandmother's closet. I didn't have time to shop for a new one, and since I got rid of most of my wardrobe before leaving Atlanta, it was either this or nothing." She turned slowly this time so that he could appreciate the full effect of the flowing fabric. "The fit isn't perfect, but I don't think anyone will notice."

The dress fit her like a damn glove. Reid shook his head again, this time to try to get her out of his head. Not that it had ever worked for him before. "Is this the surprise you have planned for your grandfather? Turning up at the ball looking the spitting image of your murdered mother? You said you wanted to provoke a reaction. This should do it."

"Yes, but it's not just for his benefit. I want to see if anyone else is provoked."

Reid frowned. "You mean the killer? Is that what this is all about? You're trying to draw him out? I'm surprised you don't have a magnolia blossom in your hair."

"I have one inside."

"I hope you're kidding."

She picked a spray of jasmine and tucked it behind her ear. "Better?"

"Not really."

She removed the spray and lifted the tiny blossoms

to her nose. "Okay, maybe I am trying to stir the pot. Listen, there's something you don't know. I talked to Ginger Vreeland today. She called on the burner phone."

Reid stared down at her in the moonlight. "Why didn't you tell me earlier?"

"Because I knew I'd be seeing you tonight. And because I didn't want you to try and talk me out of going to the ball. Reid, she knows who killed Haley Cooper."

"She said that? Who?"

"She wouldn't give me a name. She wouldn't agree to meet me, either. She's still afraid. She said Haley wasn't his first victim and if he's not caught, she won't be his last."

"So you decided to bait him?" Reid moved in closer. He wanted to take her by the arms and shake some sense into her. Not literally, of course, but what in the hell was she thinking?

"Someone has to do something. He's eluded the police for weeks, maybe even for years. If this dress or my appearance catches him by surprise, maybe he'll give himself away."

"Or maybe he'll come after you." Reid turned to scan the dark garden. The ornate dome stood silhouetted against the night sky, reminding him all too vividly of Arden's certainty that the killer had watched her from inside the summerhouse, still with her mother's blood on his hands. He turned back to Arden. "You know this is a terrible idea."

"What else are we going to do? Sit around and wait for him to kill again? If this is the same person who murdered my mother, you think he won't come after me anyway? Why do you think he left a white magnolia blossom on the summerhouse steps? He was warning me even then that he'd someday come back for me."

"You don't know that."

"Do you have a better explanation?" When he didn't reply, she shrugged. "Maybe I am off-base. Maybe Orson Lee Finch really did kill my mother. In which case, we have nothing to worry about. Let's just go tonight. Maybe we can even have a little fun. Nothing is going to happen with so many people around."

"You sound so sure of yourself," Reid said. "But it's afterwards that I'm worried about."

"I've taken precautions. Changed the locks, updated the security system. I'm safe here. Try to relax, okay? Maybe we should have a drink before we go. Just a little something to calm the nerves."

"Calm my nerves, you mean. You're as cool as a cucumber."

She gave an excited little laugh. "Not really. I feel buzzed even without anything to drink."

"You're enjoying this," he accused.

"So are you. You just don't want to admit it."

She turned and moved back inside. Reid followed, closing and locking the French doors as he stepped into the parlor. Evidently, Arden had found the key to the liquor cabinet. A crystal decanter, an ice bucket and two glasses had been arranged on a drink cart. Arden went over and picked up the tongs.

Reid watched her move in that dress. The bodice was strapless, the skirt so gossamer that when the light struck her from a certain angle, he could glimpse the silhouette of her long legs beneath.

"Sure I can't tempt you?" she asked.

He swallowed. "Maybe just a small one."

She put ice and whiskey into the glasses and held one out to him. "To partners in crime," she said.

He clinked his glass to hers. "To surviving the night." He downed the contents in one swallow. "It's getting late. Should we go?"

"In a minute." She set her glass aside untouched. "Do you mind helping me with my dress first?"

His gaze dropped appreciatively. "What's wrong with it?"

She turned her back to him. "I managed the zipper, but I couldn't reach the hook. Do you mind?"

He felt clumsy all of a sudden, but it wasn't the alcohol that made him fumble with the hook. It was the situation, the woman. All those memories.

"Do you see it?"

"Yeah." He dealt with the fastener, but his hand lingered. Her skin felt like warm satin. Reid had never touched anything so sexy.

His hands drifted to her shoulders as he bent to drop a kiss at her nape. He felt a shudder go through her, but she didn't turn, she didn't move away.

She said in a tremulous voice, "Reid?"

"Arden."

HER HEART WAS suddenly beating so hard she couldn't breathe. She took a moment to try to collect her poise before she turned to stare up at him. A mistake. How well she remembered that smoldering intensity. The tilt of his head. The knowing half smile.

She drew a shaky breath as she held his gaze. "Is this really a good idea?"

He caught her hand and pulled her to him. "Nothing about this night is a good idea. But you can't open the door looking like that and expect me not to react."

Her hands fluttered to his lapels. "We'll be late."

"When has that ever stopped us?"

Never. Not any event, not any curfew. Nothing had ever stopped them when they wanted to be together.

"We're not kids anymore," she said. "Our actions have consequences. If we do this, our working relationship will never be the same."

He slid his hands down her arms, drawing a shiver. "You said it yourself. Nothing has ever been the same since the first time we kissed in the summerhouse."

She closed her eyes briefly. "Fourteen years is a long time. What if the magic is gone?"

His arms were around her waist now, holding her close. "What if it isn't?"

She reached up to touch his cheek. He caught her hand and turned his lips into her palm. Such a soft kiss. Such an innocent touch. Arden whispered his name.

His kissed the inside of her wrist, a more sensuous seduction she could hardly imagine. She turned silently in his arms, allowing him to undo the hook he'd fastened mere seconds ago. Then he slid down the zipper and Arden took care of the rest, stepping out of the red chiffon dress and then her high heels.

She untied his bow tie, unbuttoned his collar and

slid his jacket off his shoulders. He shrugged out of the sleeves and inhaled sharply when her fingers brushed across his zipper as she tugged loose his shirt. She took his hand, leading him out of the parlor, across the foyer and up the stairs. He paused on the landing, pressing her against the banister as they kissed.

"I didn't come here expecting this," he said.

She threaded her fingers through his hair. "Are you trying to tell me you're unprepared?"

"I'm always prepared. Isn't that the Scout Motto?"

"You were never a Scout, Reid Sutton. Not even close."

He shed his shirt as they kissed their way down the hallway to her room. Moonlight filtered in from the long windows, throwing long shadows across the ceiling.

"Nothing's changed," Reid said as he glanced around the room. "I wonder if you can still shimmy down the trellis."

"I wonder if you can still climb up." She lay down on the bed and propped herself on her elbows, spreading her legs slightly as she watched him undress.

He didn't seem to mind her stare. He'd never been the least bit shy about intimacy. Nor had she, for that matter. But fourteen years was a long time. Thirty-two was not the same as eighteen.

He placed a knee on the bed and she lay back as he moved over her. Arden found herself thinking about those fourteen years, the loneliness and disappointments. The guilt and then the pride that had kept her away. She thought about their first kiss in the summerhouse, the first time they'd made love at the beach, the first time he'd told her he loved her. She could drown in those memories, good and bad, but she didn't want to lose herself to the past. Not with Reid's tongue in her mouth and his hand between her thighs. Not when that delicious pressure just kept building and building.

Slipping her hand between them, she guided him into her, then wrapped her arms and legs around him. He was leaner than she remembered. Older and more experienced. And yet he still knew her. Knew where to touch her, when to kiss her, how tightly to hold her when her body began to shudder.

And when it was over, he remembered to clasp her hand as they lay on their backs and stared up at the ceiling.

Chapter Sixteen

Reid couldn't take his eyes off Arden. He could barely keep his hands off her.

He tugged at his bow tie as he leaned a shoulder against the wall and watched her move about the room. He told himself he should be on the lookout for anyone suspicious or anything out of the ordinary. Arden's dress was bound to provoke strong reactions, but his gaze lingered as his mind drifted back to earlier in the evening.

If he'd had his way, he'd still be comfortably stretched out in her bed, but Arden had insisted they make an appearance at Mayfair House. So they'd climbed out of bed, hit the shower, and one thing had led to another. He closed his eyes briefly, imagining her hands flattened against the tile wall as she pressed her glistening body against his.

Afterward, she'd dried her damp hair, foregoing the magnolia blossom at his insistence, and touched up her makeup. Then they'd redressed like an old married couple. He'd zipped her gown and she'd straightened his bow tie. Now here they were, clothing looking the worse for wear, but totally worth it.

He brushed an invisible speck of dust from his sleeve as he forced himself to survey his surroundings.

He tried to remember the last time he'd been in Mayfair House. He and Arden had been kids, and she'd talked him into going with her because she hadn't wanted to spend the evening alone with her grandfather. Clement hadn't been pleased to see him. All through dinner, he'd stared at Reid in moody silence and as soon as the dishes had been cleared, he'd had his driver take them home.

"This place is something, isn't it? Flowers, champagne, live band. Must have set the old man back a pretty penny. And would you look at those chandeliers."

Reid turned to acknowledge his father, and lifted his gaze to the ornate ceiling. "Imported from Italy," he said.

"What?"

"The chandeliers."

"Is that so? I thought for a moment you were talking about Arden's dress. She's something, too. A real head-turner. Though I have to say, I'm a little surprised to see the two of you here together."

"Why's that?"

Boone gestured with his champagne flute. "You made a point of telling me she's not your girlfriend, remember?"

"She's not. We work together."

Boone smirked. "Do you look at all your employees that way?"

"I only have the one. And I don't think you're in any position to cast stones."

"Oh, I'm not casting stones. I'm just here to enjoy the show."

"Is Mother with you?" Reid asked pointedly.

Boone sipped his champagne. "She isn't feeling well tonight. I'm flying solo."

"Just the way you like it."

"Let's make a deal. You stay out of my private life and I'll stay out of yours."

Reid shrugged. "Whatever you say."

Boone set his glass on a passing waiter's tray. "Since you and Arden have only a working relationship, you won't mind if I ask her to dance."

"Knock yourself out," Reid said. "But don't be surprised if she wants to lead."

"I think I can handle Arden Mayfair."

"Yeah. That's what I used to think, too."

ARDEN HAD FORGOTTEN how charming Boone Sutton could be. Handsome and debonair, and always just a little too smooth in her book. She was surprised when he had asked her to dance. She used the opportunity to glance around the room as they moved over the floor. Curious eyes met hers. She nodded to acquaintances and smiled at her uncle, who stood watching from one of the arched doorways.

"Strange guy," Boone muttered.

"My uncle? I would say he comes by it honestly,

wouldn't you? My grandfather is nothing if not eccentric." Her gaze strayed again to the edge of the dance floor where she'd last seen Reid. He'd disappeared, but she couldn't imagine he'd gone far. She turned her attention back to Boone. "Reid told me about your theory. You think my mother wasn't Clement Mayfair's biological child. That would explain a lot, actually."

"Well, it is just a theory." He spun her unexpectedly. Arden had to concentrate to keep up.

"You knew my grandmother well," she said. "She never confided in you?"

"Evelyn kept things close to the vest. She wasn't the type to air dirty laundry even among friends. I don't pretend to know what went on in this house before she divorced Clement, but I can say with utter confidence that she would have done anything to protect her family. You and your mother were everything to her."

"What about her son?"

"As I said, Calvin is a strange fellow. Always has been." A frown flickered as if he'd thought of something unpleasant. "I was surprised to hear that you'd moved back to Charleston. I thought you were done with this city for good. Maybe that would have been for the best."

"For Reid's sake?"

He hesitated. "For your own. These are troubling times. Reid has gotten himself into something of a bind, it seems. It would be a shame if you became entangled in that mess, too."

"You surely don't think he had anything to do with Haley Cooper's murder."

A shadow flitted across his expression. "Of course, I don't. But he put himself into a position of being blackmailed by the likes of Dave Brody. A man in Reid's position has to be more careful. Someone like Brody is always looking to take advantage."

"Maybe Brody isn't the real problem," Arden said. "He claims someone powerful is trying to frame Reid. Maybe that same person paid Haley to spike Reid's drink."

Boone froze for half a beat. "What are you talking about?"

"Reid didn't tell you? She slipped something into his drink that night at the bar. Why would she do that to a perfect stranger unless someone paid her? From what I understand, she liked the finer things in life."

"She wasn't—"

"She wasn't what?"

"Nothing."

No sooner had the conversation fizzled than something the shop owner had revealed came back to Arden. Haley had been seeing someone older, someone wealthy. Someone who guarded his privacy. Because he was married?

She told herself she was being ridiculous. Any number of men in the city fit that description, many of them here at the ball. Boone Sutton was a lot of things, but he was no murderer.

How do you know?

Her gaze met her uncle's again, moved on and then came back. He couldn't seem to take his eyes off her, and no wonder—he'd painted her mother in this very dress.

Suddenly the walls started to close in and Arden wished she'd heeded Reid's warning. Coming here to-night had been a very bad idea.

The music ended, but Boone's arm seemed to tighten around her waist. "Something wrong?"

"No, of course, not." Arden backed away. "Thank you for the dance, but I think I'll go find Reid now."

She wandered through the house, avoiding anyone who looked familiar while she searched for Reid. The terrace doors in the library were open and she stepped through, scanning the silhouettes that lingered in the garden. A cool breeze blew in from the harbor, stirring her hair and fanning her dress. She turned to go back inside, but someone blocked her path.

Her heart beat a startled tattoo as she stared up at her grandfather. He had always intimidated and unsettled her; however, she was a grown woman now. No reason to fear him.

"Grandfather," she said on a breath. "I didn't hear you come up."

He said nothing for the longest moment, just stood there in the dark staring down at her.

"I'm looking for Reid," she said. "Have you seen him?"

"I have not."

His voice was like a cold wind down her back, devoid of warmth or affection. Hard to believe that he had actually warned Reid away from her. Why would he even care?

"This is quite an event." She waved a hand toward the terrace doors. "You've outdone yourself."

"As have you."

She suspected he was talking about the dress, and she pretended not to understand. "I was surprised to hear that you were hosting the Mayor's Ball this year. Somehow it doesn't seem your kind of thing."

Moonlight reflected off his glasses as he tilted his head slightly. "And just what is my kind of thing?"

"You never used to like company, much less a crowd. But then, I've been away for a long time. People change, I suppose."

"You haven't. This is exactly the kind of stunt you would have pulled as a child. You're an adult now. I had high hopes that you would outgrow your unseemly tendencies. But you're too much like your mother. Evelyn always had to be the center of the universe. You apparently have her morals, too."

A chill shot down Arden's backbone. "Evelyn was my grandmother. I'm Arden."

"Go home, girl. Don't come back until you've learned how to dress and behave like a lady."

"Grandfather—"

A commotion from inside the house drew their attention. Arden trailed her grandfather inside as he headed toward the raised voices. The music had stopped and everyone seemed suspended in shock. Arden followed their gazes. Detective Graham and two uniformed cops had surrounded Reid.

Arden rushed toward them. "What's going on?"

One of the officers put up his hand. "Stand back, miss."

"Reid?"

"There's nothing to worry about," he said in a calm voice. "Detective Graham has a few questions that apparently can only be answered at police headquarters."

"This couldn't have waited until the morning?" Clement demanded.

The two men exchanged glances.

The detective said in a conciliatory tone, "My apologies for the disturbance. We felt this a matter of some urgency."

"Oh, I'm sure you did." Boone materialized at Arden's side. "I'm sure the urgency had nothing at all to do with the press being here tonight or the fact that your picture will likely be on the front page of the newspaper tomorrow."

The detective's expression had grown cold with contempt. "I'm just doing my job."

"Is he under arrest?"

"We just have a few questions."

Boone turned to Reid. "Don't say a word. Not one word. You hear me?"

"I know what I'm doing," Reid said. "Let's just get this over with. No need to ruin everyone else's evening."

They all traipsed outside to a waiting squad car. After another few minutes of discussion, Reid willingly climbed into the back and the car pulled away.

Boone waited for the valet service to fetch his car while Arden called a cab.

"I hope you called that cab to take you home," Boone said.

"Of course not. I'm going to police headquarters."

"That's not a good idea. You heard the detective. Reid isn't under arrest. Let's make sure we keep it that way."

"Someone is trying to set him up," Arden said. "We can't let that happen."

"Which is why I need you to do something for me." He pulled her away from the crowd that had assembled on the steps and lowered his voice. "Go to Reid's place right now and make sure everything is clean."

Arden frowned up at him. "What are you talking about?"

"Use your head. You think a dirty cop like Graham is above planting evidence?"

"But—" Arden started to protest being sidelined. If nothing else, she wanted to offer Reid her moral support. Then she thought of the note that had been left in his closet by the intruder. What if Graham had somehow managed to plant the murder weapon inside Reid's house?

She swallowed back her panic and nodded. "Okay. But you take care of this. You get him out of there, you hear me?"

ARDEN HAD THE DRIVER drop her off at the end of the block, and she hurried along the shadowy street to Reid's house. Glancing over her shoulder, she let herself in and locked the door behind her. She moved quickly from room to room, drawing the blinds at all the front windows before she turned on the lights.

She started the task in his office and worked her way through the house, combing the obvious places and then looking for more obscure hiding places. When a third search turned up nothing, she had the unsettling notion that maybe evidence had been planted elsewhere. Someplace less likely yet still incriminating, like the summerhouse at Berdeaux Place.

She called another cab and paced the front porch until the car arrived. Five minutes later she was home. She let herself in, locked the door behind her and turned off the security system. Then she headed through the parlor to the French doors.

Her hand froze on the latch. Her mother's cereus had bloomed during the evening. Someone had cut off every last flower and chopped the petals to bits with her grandmother's antique katana.

Shredded them in a rage, Arden thought.

The katana had been tossed aside in the grass. The sword had been in its usual place when Arden and Reid had left for the ball. Someone had been inside the house. How was that possible? The alarm had been set, the front door locked tight…

She whirled, her focus moving across the room to the foyer. Someone was coming down the stairs, slowly, deliberately, taking his time as he anticipated the encounter…

Arden reacted on instinct. She went out the French doors and grabbed the katana. The lush, heady fragrance of the destroyed blooms filled her nostrils. The moon was up, flooding the terrace and garden with hazy light. She dove for the shadows, concealing herself as best she could as she rushed toward the side entrance. The wrought-iron gate had been padlocked from the other side and the low-hanging limb that she had once used to propel herself over the wall had long since been cut away.

She was trapped in the garden. No way out except to go back through the house.

Whirling, she moved down the path toward the summerhouse. She couldn't hide there, of course. He would surely look for her inside. She broke off a sprig of jasmine and tossed it to the ground and then another. Deliberate breadcrumbs. Then she plunged deep into the shadowy jungle of her grandmother's garden and hunkered down out of sight.

He came along the path, calling out to her. "Come out, come out wherever you are!"

Arden pressed herself back into the bushes, clapping a hand over her mouth to silence her breath. She knew who he was now. Knew why the Twilight Killer had come back for her.

"Did you really think you could keep me out of Berdeaux Place by changing the locks?" he called. "Did you really think I wouldn't have my own way in without tripping the alarm? I know every square inch of that house. Every nook and cranny. Every single one of your little hiding places."

Her uncle was at the summerhouse steps now. He climbed the stairs slowly, a kitchen knife glinting in his hand. He turned at the top and surveyed the garden before ducking inside. Arden shifted her weight, positioning herself to make a dash for the house, but he came back out too quickly, pausing again on the steps as his gaze seemed to zero in on her hiding place.

"I used to come here all the time after Mother left me. I'd sneak inside and stand at Camille's bedside while she slept. Mother caught me once. She told Father, and the next day he sent me away to boarding school. Military school came next and then university. They did what they could to keep us separated. Did you know that's why Mother took Camille away from Mayfair House? She was afraid for her. Afraid of me. Her own son."

Arden was trembling now, picturing him creeping through the house. Watching her mother sleep. Watching *her*.

"That night when I saw her in the garden wearing the red dress, I knew it had to be her. She would be my first. The waiting became unbearable so I came back a few days later and did what I had to do. You saw me that night, here in the summerhouse. I left a magnolia blossom just for you. Do you remember?"

Arden clutched the handle of her grandmother's sword. She'd put her bag down with her phone when she first came in. She couldn't call Reid or the police for help. She was on her own. She had to somehow get inside the house. Lock the doors. Find her phone...

But what good would that do when he had a secret way in?

"I have something else for you tonight," he said. "I

know you can see me. I know you're close. I can hear your heartbeat. Can you hear mine?"

Yes, yes, there it was, a throbbing that filled her senses until she wanted to press her hands to her ears and scream. She knew on some level that it was her own heartbeat thudding in her ears, and yet she could have sworn the cacophony filled the garden just as it had on the night of her mother's death.

"Look what I have for you, Arden."

She peered through the bushes, wanting to glance away but mesmerized by the red magnolia petals he scattered across the summerhouse steps. The breeze lifted one and carried it toward her. The crimson kiss of death.

"That night was magical," he said. "So thrilling I can hardly believe it actually happened. The others that came afterward were just pale imitations. I thought I'd never again experience such ecstasy until you walked into Mayfair House tonight wearing that red dress." He came down the steps and stood in the moonlight, staring through the bushes straight at her. "Come out, Arden. Come see what else I have for you."

She stood, hiding the katana in the folds of her gown. "You killed my mother. You killed all those other women, leaving their children motherless, and then you let an innocent man rot in prison for your crimes."

"I'm a Mayfair," he said, as if that were the only explanation needed.

He moved toward her slowly, a cat closing in on his prey. Arden stood her ground, gripping the handle of the hidden weapon until he was almost upon her. He pounced, more quickly than she had anticipated. She swung the katana, slicing him across the lower rib cage, wounding but not felling him. He staggered back, eyes wild, expression contorted as he gripped his side and took several deep breaths.

Arden sprinted away from him, nearly tripping as the bushes caught the gossamer layers of her dress. She kicked off her shoes and ran barefoot toward the house, spurred on by fear and pure adrenaline. She had almost made it to the terrace when he tackled her from behind and she landed face-first on the stone pathway.

Dazed and breathless, she tried to fight him off. The blood from his wound soaked her dress and dripped onto the grass as he pulled her deeper into the garden, to the exact spot where he had taken her mother's life.

She'd lost the katana, Arden realized. She dug her fingernails into the ground, trying to stop his momentum, while on and on he dragged her. She kicked and writhed, but he seemed to have supernatural strength. Bloodlust drove him. Years and years of pent up rage and resentment.

Pinning her arms with his knees, he rose over her, backlit by the moon. He gazed down at her as he must have stared down at her mother. He lifted the knife overhead, preparing for a thrust that would take her life just as he had taken her mother's.

She heard voices. Someone called out her name. A shadow appeared in the garden and then another.

One of the shadows tackled her uncle, knocking him back into the bushes. The two men fought viciously. The knife struck home, slashing Reid's arm. He grunted in pain and grabbed Calvin's wrist, holding the weapon at bay. Arden looked around desperately for the katana. She grabbed it, stumbled forward. Before she could strike, a shot rang out. Her uncle froze for a split second and then he toppled backward to the ground, his eyes open as he stared blindly at the moon.

Arden rushed to Reid's side, checking his wound and holding him close. They both gazed up at Boone Sutton, who still clutched his weapon. He said to no one in particular, "Sometimes the mad dog has to be put down."

Then he turned and walked away, giving them a moment of privacy before the police descended once again on Berdeaux Place.

Chapter Seventeen

"Orson Lee Finch will soon be a free man," Reid said the next day as he reclined back in his chair. His feet were propped on his desk, his arm in a sling. Everything considered, he looked cool and collected.

Arden was seated in the chair opposite his desk. She was still strung out from the night's events and from the hours she'd spent at police headquarters. It would take a long time before she felt normal again, but at least something good had come from tragedy. "I read that his daughter and grown grandchildren will be there to greet him when he walks through the gate. I can hardly imagine what they all must be feeling right now. If only I'd recognized my uncle that night. If only I'd been able to stop him."

"None of this is your fault," Reid said.

"I know. I was just a child when Mother died. Whatever I saw that night... I couldn't make sense of it."

"Boone knew. Or at least he suspected. That's why he helped Ginger Vreeland leave town. Calvin had roughed her up, and she was afraid he'd come back and kill her. He says he told the police, but Clement

Mayfair is a powerful man. You don't go after his son unless you have irrefutable proof."

"Grandmother knew, too," Arden said. "That's why she took my mother away from that house. Why she left her son behind. She knew even then what he was."

"What a terrible thing to have to live with," Reid said.

"She was never the same after my mother's death. None of us were." Arden fell silent. "Why do you think he killed Haley Cooper? She wasn't a single mother. She didn't fit his usual profile. Why her?"

Reid shrugged. "We can only speculate. She'd had a brief relationship with Boone. Calvin probably used her and Dave Brody to set me up. It was never about a conviction. He wanted to cast doubt on my father's character so that if he came forward with his suspicions, it would seem as though he was casting aspersions to clear his own son."

"My uncle must have started planning this as soon as he heard I was coming back."

"That's why your grandfather wanted Berdeaux Place so badly. He thought if he took that house away from you, you'd have no reason to stay in Charleston."

"And that's why he warned you away from me," Arden said.

"For all the good it did."

She got up and rounded the desk, leaning against the side as she gazed down at Reid. "In all the commotion, we haven't had time to discuss us."

"What's there to discuss?" He took her arm and

pulled her down to his lap. "I let you go once without a fight. I'm not about to do that again."

"You don't see me running, do you?"

"Partners in crime?"

"Partners in crime." She settled in, taking care not to jostle his wounded arm as she reached up and touched his cheek. "But you still have to say it."

He smiled. "Why do I have to say it? You already know how I feel."

"Because a girl needs to hear it."

"All right then." He held her close. "I love you, Arden Mayfair. I've loved you from the moment I first laid eyes on you, and I'll love you until my last day on this earth. How's that?"

"That'll do just fine," she said with a sigh.

* * * * *

#1869 IRON WILL
Cardwell Ranch: Montana Legacy • by B.J. Daniels
Hank Savage is certain his girlfriend was murdered, so he hires private investigator Frankie Brewster to pretend to be his lover and help him find the killer. Before long, they are in over their heads...and head over heels.

#1870 THE STRANGER NEXT DOOR
A Winchester, Tennessee Thriller • by Debra Webb
After spending eight years in jail for a crime she didn't commit, Cecelia Winters is eager to find out who really killed her father, a religious fanatic and doomsday prepper. In order to discover the truth, she must work with Deacon Ross, a man who is certain Cecelia killed his mentor and partner.

#1871 SECURITY RISK
The Risk Series: A Bree and Tanner Thriller • by Janie Crouch
A few months ago, Tanner Dempsey saved Bree Daniels, but suddenly they find themselves back in danger when Tanner's past comes back to haunt the couple. Will the pair be able to stop the criminal before it's too late?

#1872 ADIRONDACK ATTACK
Protectors at Heart • by Jenna Kernan
When Detective Dalton Stevens follows his estranged wife, Erin, to the Adirondack Mountains in an effort to win her back, neither of them expects to become embroiled in international intrigue. Then they are charged with delivering classified information to Homeland Security.

#1873 PERSONAL PROTECTION
by Julie Miller
Ivan Mostek knows two things: someone wants him dead and a member of his inner circle is betraying him. With undercover cop Carly Valentine by his side, can he discover the identity of the traitor before it's too late?

#1874 NEW ORLEANS NOIR
by Joanna Wayne
Helena Cosworth is back in New Orleans to sell her grandmother's house. Suddenly, she is a serial killer's next target, and she is forced to turn to Detective Hunter Bergeron, a man she once loved and lost, for help. Together, will they be able to stop the elusive French Kiss Killer?

Get 4 FREE REWARDS!

We'll send you 2 FREE Books plus 2 FREE Mystery Gifts.

Harlequin Intrigue® books feature heroes and heroines that confront and survive danger while finding themselves irresistibly drawn to one another.

FREE
Value Over
$20

YES! Please send me 2 FREE Harlequin Intrigue® novels and my 2 FREE gifts (gifts are worth about $10 retail). After receiving them, if I don't wish to receive any more books, I can return the shipping statement marked "cancel." If I don't cancel, I will receive 6 brand-new novels every month and be billed just $4.99 each for the regular-print edition or $5.74 each for the larger-print edition in the U.S., or $5.74 each for the regular-print edition or $6.49 each for the larger-print edition in Canada. That's a savings of at least 12% off the cover price! It's quite a bargain! Shipping and handling is just 50¢ per book in the U.S. and 75¢ per book in Canada.* I understand that accepting the 2 free books and gifts places me under no obligation to buy anything. I can always return a shipment and cancel at any time. The free books and gifts are mine to keep no matter what I decide.

Choose one: ☐ **Harlequin Intrigue®**
Regular-Print
(182/382 HDN GMYW)

☐ **Harlequin Intrigue®**
Larger-Print
(199/399 HDN GMYW)

Name (please print)

Address   Apt. #

City   State/Province   Zip/Postal Code

Mail to the **Reader Service:**
IN U.S.A.: P.O. Box 1341, Buffalo, NY 14240-8531
IN CANADA: P.O. Box 603, Fort Erie, Ontario L2A 5X3

Want to try 2 free books from another series! Call 1-800-873-8635 or visit www.ReaderService.com.

*Terms and prices subject to change without notice. Prices do not include sales taxes, which will be charged (if applicable) based on your state or country of residence. Canadian residents will be charged applicable taxes. Offer not valid in Quebec. This offer is limited to one order per household. Books received may not be as shown. Not valid for current subscribers to Harlequin Intrigue books. All orders subject to approval. Credit or debit balances in a customer's account(s) may be offset by any other outstanding balance owed by or to the customer. Please allow 4 to 6 weeks for delivery. Offer available while quantities last.

Your Privacy—The Reader Service is committed to protecting your privacy. Our Privacy Policy is available online at www.ReaderService.com or upon request from the Reader Service. We make a portion of our mailing list available to reputable third parties that offer products we believe may interest you. If you prefer that we not exchange your name with third parties, or if you wish to clarify or modify your communication preferences, please visit us at www.ReaderService.com/consumerschoice or write to us at Reader Service Preference Service, P.O. Box 9062, Buffalo, NY 14240-9062. Include your complete name and address.

HI19R2

It wasn't long before they were arriving at the ranch. He grabbed her overnight bag, and they walked inside.

"We both need to get a few hours' sleep," he said. "I'll take the couch and you can have the bed."

She walked toward the bedroom but turned at the door. "Come with me. Just to sleep together like before." Those big green eyes studied him as she reached her hand out toward him.

There was nothing he wanted more than to curl up with her in his bed. But with his anger and frustration so close to the surface, he couldn't discount the fact that he might wake up swinging. The thought of Bree being the recipient of his night terrors made him break out into a cold sweat.

"Never mind," she said quickly, misreading his hesitation, hand falling back to her side. "You don't have to."

Damn it, he'd rather never sleep again than see that wounded look in her eyes from something he'd done.

He stepped toward her. "I want to. Trust me, there's nothing I want more. But…I just don't want to take a chance on waking you up if I get called back in to Risk Peak early." That was at least a partial truth.

The haunted look fell away from her eyes, and a shy smile broke on her face. "I don't mind. I'll take a shorter amount of sleep if it means I get to sleep next to you."

He would have given her anything in the world to keep that sweet smile on her face. He took her hand, and they walked into the bedroom together.

They took turns changing into sleep clothes in the bathroom, then got into the bed together. The act was so innocent and yet so intimate.

Tanner rolled over onto his side and pulled Bree's back against his front. He breathed in the sweet scent of her hair as her head rested in the crook of his elbow. His other arm wrapped loosely around her waist.

She was out within minutes, her smaller body relaxing against him, trusting him to shelter and protect her while she slept. Tanner wouldn't betray that trust, even if that meant protecting her against himself.

Besides, sleeping was overrated when he could be awake and feeling every curve that had been haunting his dreams for months pressed against him.

Definitely worth it.

Don't miss
Security Risk *by Janie Crouch,*
available August 2019 wherever
Harlequin® Intrigue *books and ebooks are sold.*

www.Harlequin.com

HIEXP0719